A King Production presents…

MOVIE EDITION

The Story of Precious Cummings

a novel

JOY DEJA KING

ISBN 10: 1-958834-88-2
ISBN 13: 978-1958834886
Cover concept by Joy Deja King
Cover model: Joy Deja King

Cover layout and graphic design by: www. anitaart79.wixsite.com/anita
Typesetting: anita.art79@gmail.com
Library of Congress Cataloging-in-Publication Data;
King, Deja Joy
For complete Library of Congress Copyright info visit
www.joydejaking.com

P.O. Box 912, Collierville, TN 38027

A King Production and the above portrayal log are trademarks of A King Production LLC

This Book is Dedicated To My:

Family, Readers, and Supporters. I LOVE you guys so much. Please believe that!!

—Joy Deja King

I Do Not Fear The Fire
I Am The Fire...

~ Precious Cummings ~

A KING PRODUCTION
Bitch
The Story Of Precious Cummings
MOVIE EDITION
A Novel
JOY DEJA KING

Started From The Bottom

Coming from nothing and having nothing are two different things. Yeah, I came from nothing, but I was determined to have it all. And how couldn't I?

I exploded into this world when hood rich wasn't an afterthought, but the only thought. You turn on the television or go on social media and every nigga is iced out with an exotic whip, surrounded by a bitch in a G-string, bundles down to her ass, poppin' that booty. So, the chicks in videos were dropping it like it's hot for the rappers, singers and athletes, while the bitches around my way were dropping it for our own superstars. Dealing with a street nigga on a legendary drug kingpin status was like being Beyonce herself on Jigga Man's arm. A bitch like me was thirsty for that. I'd been on some type of hustle since I was in pampers.

I grew up in the grimiest Brooklyn projects. It was worse than being in prison because you knew there was something better out there; you just didn't know how to get it. You never saw green grass or flowers blooming. Instead of looking up to teachers, lawyers, or doctors, you worshipped the local drug dealers who hustled to survive and escape their existence. Even as a little girl, I knew I wanted more out of life. Somehow hustling was in my blood.

First, I hustled for my moms' attention because she was too busy turning tricks to pay me any mind. I never knew who my daddy was, so while my mom was fucking in her bedroom, I would wait outside the door with my legs crossed, holding my favorite teddy bear in one arm as I sucked my thumb. When the tricks would come out, I would look at them with puppy-dog eyes and ask, "Are you, my daddy?" The question would freak them out so badly they'd toss me a few dollars so I would shut the fuck up.

One day when I was five, my mother was looking for something in my drawers, she came across a bunch of fives and tens and some twenties. The total was five hundred and some change. Of course, she wanted to know where all the money came from. When I told her that the money came from her business clients (that's what my mom called them), she lit up. She tossed me up in the air and said, "Baby, you my good luck charm. I knew one day you'd make me some money."

On that rare occasion she showed me mad love.

As young as I was, I equated my mother's newfound interest in me with love. From that moment on, I learned how to hustle for my moms' attention, by providing her with money.

Somehow, my moms' customers never messed with or tried to fondle me. I think it's because even as a little girl I had this darkness in my eyes, that said, "Don't fuck wit' me."

By the time I was fifteen with all the tricks my mom's pulled, we were still dead ass broke, living in the projects. She couldn't save a dime because with hooking comes drugging and my mom's stayed high. I guess that's all you can do to escape the nightmare of having all types of nasty, greasy fat motherfuckers pounding your back out every damn day. The characters that I saw coming in and out of our apartment were enough to make me want to sew up my pussy so nobody could get between my legs, but my mother would soon change all that.

One day, I was sitting at home watching a weekly vlog on YouTube from one of my favorite social media influencers. She was doing beauty maintenance and self-care. I was completely caught up that I almost didn't hear my mother's bedroom door open. I heard the floor squeak and immediately turned off the television. Without a word, I started giving the living room a lick and a promise. I emptied several full ashtrays, picked up the dirty glasses scattered about the floor and wiped off the cocktail table.

Out of the corner of my eye, I watched my mother stare at me for a few minutes. She had the strangest look on her face. She was holding a bottle of whiskey in one hand and a cigarette in the other. My mother was only 33 but living a reckless life filled with drugs and heavy drinking had taken its toll. With unkept hair, poor hygiene, and a nasty disposition, most of the time I couldn't stand being around her. There was no trace of the once curvy beauty that every hood chick envied. Her once long, wavy hair was now thin and straggly. The one-time ghetto queen was just a bag of bones that you wouldn't even recognize unless you stared deeply into the green eyes she inherited from her father.

It was the middle of the afternoon, and she was just waking up, still wearing her dingy nightgown, blowing smoke in the air. She held on tightly to her cigarette, staring at me as if I was a reminder of what she used to be in her prime.

"Precious, you sure are growing up to be a pretty girl." I stayed silent and continued picking up clothes that were scattered on the floor and then started sweeping. "Didn't you hear what yo' mama said?"

"Yes, I heard you."

"Well, you betta say thank you."

"Thank you, ma."

"You welcome, baby."

My mother walked over to the couch and sat down with her legs spread open. She took one last long pull from her cigarette and put it out in the ash-

tray. She then took a swig from the whiskey bottle. The alcohol was spilling down her chin.

"Baby, you know that your mother is getting up there in age. I can't put it down like I used to. So baby, I was thinking maybe you need to start helping me out a little more."

Her comment made me pause and frown up my face. "Help you out more how? I basically give you my whole paycheck."

"Like I said, yo' mama can't put it down like I used to."

That bullshit made me stop sweeping the floor and I stared directly in my mother's eyes.

"What does any of that have to do wit' me? I barely go to school as it is because what was supposed to be a parttime job at the car detailing shop is more like fulltime. Damn near every cent I make, goes in your pocket to pay bills."

"Baby, that little job you got ain't bringing home no money. It's just enough to maintain. I'm talking about getting a real job."

I started sweeping the floor again wanting to ignore the foolishness coming out her mouth.

"Ma, I'm fifteen. It's only so many jobs I can get and so much money I can make. My boss not even supposed to give me all the hours she has me doing at the shop. That's why she pays me off the books."

"Precious, as pretty as you are you can be making thousands of dollars."

"Doing what? What job you know is going to pay a fifteen-year-old high school student thousands of dollars?"

"The oldest profession in the book...sex."

"You said that as if you asking me to do something as innocent as baking cookies for a living. You done lost yo' damn mind. What you tryna be now—my pimp!"

"You betta watch yo' mouth, little girl. I'm yo' mama. Don't forget that."

"Don't you forget it! You must have if you asking me to sell my ass so I can take care of you."

"Not me—us. Shit, I took care of yo' ass for the last fifteen years. Breaking my back and wearing out my pussy to provide us with a good life."

"This is what you call a good life?" I twirled the wooden handle of the broom around the living room as I looked at the cluttered two-bedroom apartment. The hardwood floors were heavily scratched with a few roaches crawling near the entrance to the kitchen. Visible holes in the walls and decaying window frames with cracks in the glass. My mother stood up real defiant like and pointed her finger at me.

"You listen here, a lot of these children around this way don't even have a place to stay. It might not be much to yo' ungrateful ass but it's mine."

"That's a lie. You don't even own this raggedy-ass apartment." We stared each other down for a few moments because I wasn't budging. "Sorry to disappoint

you, but I'm not following in your footsteps by selling my pussy to some low-down niggas for money," I made clear then shrugged my shoulders brushing the bull-shit off.

"Well then you betta start looking for someplace to live, 'cause I can't support both of us."

"You tryna tell me you would put me out on the streets!"

"You ain't leaving me a choice, Precious. If you can't bring home some extra money, then I'll have to rent out your bedroom to pay the bills."

"Who gon' pay for that piece of shit of a room?"

"Listen, I ain't 'bout to sit up here and argue wit' you. Either you start bringing home some money or find another place to live. It's up to you. But if you don't give me a thousand dollars by the first of the month, I need you out by the second."

"How the fuck am I supposed to come up wit' a thousand dollars by the first of the month?"

"I told you. You betta start using what's between your legs." My trifling mother then cut her eyes at my vagina before her skeletal body disappeared into her dungeon of a bedroom. She was practically sentencing me to the homeless shelter. There was no way I could give her a thousand dollars a month unless I dropped out of high school and worked fulltime at the detail shop. But what made this so fucked up was this had nothing to do with the monthly bills because she had subsidized housing and received plenty of other help from the government. My mother basically wanted me to pay for her out-of-control drug habit.

Because the street life had beaten my mother, she wanted to beat me over the head with bullshit. But I refused to let that happen. I would hustle up that money, but I would do it my way. I was going to pick and choose who was able to play between my legs. My job at the car detailing shop was the perfect place for me to start. Nothing but top-of-the-line hustlers parlayed through, and one of them would be mine.

Get That Bag

I arrived at work focused on what I called the get money mission. Since time wasn't on my side, I only had a week to scope out all the dudes that were coming in and out the detailing shop. I was carefully seeking out the perfect mark. He had to be cute, paid and hopefully, willing to spend his money freely. In two more weeks, it was going to be the first and my mother was still threatening to throw me the fuck out.

While standing in the entryway of the car detailing shop, I zoomed in on a cutie getting out a drop top BMW. After tracking how he moved for a few minutes, I decided he was a potential target.

"Good morning!" I said holding the door open for my boss before we both headed inside.

"My favorite girl has arrived for work!" Bree smiled. "It's Saturday, so you know it will be a nonstop busy day."

"As always, I'm ready." I stated being extra bubbly with Bree. I walked behind the register counter
stand and started stacking some car magazines neat-
ly on top of one another as I prepared to get some info
on my target. "Bree, who that cutie in the drop top
Beamer?"

"Oh, that's Azar. He moved here from Philly, why
you ask?"

"I ain't never seen him 'round here before, and I
wanted to know who he was."

I peeped Bree side eyeing me. I knew she was
probably curious as to why I was asking about him
since I never showed any interest in the customers.
She stood in front of the stand continuing to eye me.

"Is that the only reason?" she pried.

"Actually, to keep it real wit' you, Bree, I'm looking for a man and the guy in the BMW might be the
one."

"Looking for a man? One of the reasons you've
been my best receptionist is because you weren't distracted by none of these hustlers that came through
here. Why the sudden change?"

"I rather not get into all that, but I will tell you I
really don't have a choice. I need money and dealing
wit' a dude who is gettin' paper seems to be the only
way to make it happen."

"You are much too young to have those types of
worries. I can give you a raise, Precious."

I folded my arms and let out a deep sigh. "Bree,

unless that raise is a few thousand dollars then it ain't gonna do me no good." Shit, I figured if I had to give my mother a thousand dollars a month, I might as well make a few more for my own personal use.

"I don't know what you need all that money for, but if you wanna fuck with Azar or any baller, then let me school you on a few things. I need to ask you a question first. Are you looking to play the long game or are you looking for fast cash?"

"Fast cash."

"You're young, so what's your sex game like?"

I debated if I wanted to tell Bree I was a virgin. "It could use some work. Why?"

Bree leaned forward on the counter. "I mean if you want one of these hustlers out here to spend some serious paper on you in a speedy manner, you gotta learn to sex them *really* good. You're a beautiful girl, so attracting their attention is the easy part. Having him willing to spend the way you want; your sex game must be on point. Just giving you something to consider. Personally, I think you should focus on school and work. But if you plan on putting yourself out here, make sure you do it right." Bree gave me a cautionary glare and walked back outside.

If there was anybody's advice I trusted; it was Bree. She was like the forever hot girl but who was also wise like your favorite Auntie. Although I didn't know her exact age, I knew Bree was old enough to be my mother, yet she still maintained her looks and was street savvy from her time dealing with major drug dealers.

Bree was right. If I really wanted to land a hustler and get him to spend money with the quickness, I had to get my fuck game in order. The funny thing was from watching my mother selling her ass all my life, it turned me off from sex. I was probably the last virgin in my hood. I definitely needed a lot of work, and I needed to find someone that I could practice on before I actually put myself out there and tried to land a baller. One thing I promised myself, that no matter what, I would never let myself go out like my mother. I would play men; they would never play me.

By the end of the week, I had narrowed down my search to three dudes. The nigga Azar was actually my first choice, because not only did he have the drop-top beamer, but he also came through in a Range and a big body Benz. He was fine as fuck too. But Bree forewarned me that although the nigga was young, he was also gangsta. You couldn't half-ass him. He wasn't just giving his money to any random bitch like some goofy niggas do, which meant my game had to be tight.

Since I still hadn't learned how to fuck, I was a little skeptical about trying my hand with him. The other two guys were some come up type dudes. They were always trying to get at me. They would hit me off

with a hundred-dollar tip when they paid. I knew both of them would lace me with some real paper if I gave them some. Plus, they were only a'ight in the looks department. They would pay me just so they could have eye candy in the passenger seat of their car, which made them easy marks, but I wanted Azar. Something about him made me feel he would not only stimulate my pockets but also my body. Once I determined Azar would be the one to fill my bag with cash, now all I had to do was find the right guy to sharpen my nonexistent sex skills.

On a rare day of going to school, on my way home, I peeped my neighbor Jamal. He was a real straight-laced type of dude and one of the few of us in the neighborhood who had a mother and father living under the same roof. They were a hard-working couple, but due to their lack of education, they were barely getting by. Jamal was supposed to be their savior.

See, Jamal was a certified genius. He was only in ninth grade but taking twelfth grade classes. There was no doubt he would get a full scholarship to any college of his choosing. All the top prep schools around the country wanted him to attend their school, but Jamal's parents refused to let him leave home. They felt he was too young and would get brainwashed in the white man's world—their words. So, he just took all advanced classes in preparation for his college departure.

"What's up, Jamal?" I walked up beside him. His eyes damn near popped out of his thick-rimmed bifocals. That didn't surprise me, because we had been living next to one another our entire lives and I never spoke more than two words to him besides, "Boy move."

"Precious." He paused for a minute, looking at me, not sure if he heard me correctly.

"Yeah, what's up, Jamal?" I asked in a sweet voice. "How are you doing?"

"I'm doing okay. Just on my way home to study for an exam I have in a couple of days." I couldn't front, the dedication that dude had for his books was crazy. I had to admit I somewhat admired the ghetto nerd.

"That's cool. I was wondering if maybe we could study together. I've been working so hard at my part-time job that I fell behind on a lot of work. I was hoping you could help me catch up. I know how smart you are."

"You want to study with me?" Jamal sounded stunned. "But you don't even like me."

I linked my arm around Jamal's arm. Getting close to him. "Jamal, that's not true. I just always got so much to deal with. Work, school and of course you and everyone else in the building knows what my mom's got going on."

There was an awkward silence before Jamal spoke up. "Sure, I'll help you. When do you want to study?"

"How about today?"

Jamal hesitated for a moment. "I don't know, Precious. I really need to study for my test. How about Wednesday?"

"Jamal, you know you'll ace that test with your eyes closed. I really need you today." Jamal continued to be hesitant, so I moved even closer, trying to encourage him to see things my way. I ran my hand softly down his arm. "Please, Jamal, you do want me to pass?"

"But..." I stopped him before he could protest.

"No buts, Jamal." I put my index finger over his lips. I had to get my money up, so if I needed to be a little aggressive with my approach, then so be it.

Sex Is My Weapon

The persuasion in my voice and gentle touch finally made Jamal fall in line. We were now sitting at the desk in his room. Jamal's parents were at work, so we were home alone. I was on the clock, so I decided it was time to makes my move.

"Jamal, have you ever had sex before?"

"Excuse me?" he nervously fidgeted with his book.

"You heard me. Has your little thing ever gotten wet off some coochie juices?"

I wanted to laugh at how uncomfortable I was making Jamal with my unfiltered questions, but I also didn't want to make him so nervous he was unable to perform. He continued to squirm in his chair.

"Precious, we're supposed to be studying, not talking about sex."

"I know, but there's a reason for this. See, I'm a

virgin," I announced, reaching over and closing the book Jamal was reading. "I want to date this guy, but he's used to dealing with experienced women. If I tried to get with him and he knew I was a virgin, he would laugh at me like I was some little girl. I need to be able to hold my own when we get down to it."

"Interesting, but why are you telling me?" Jamal opened the book back up trying to stay on task.

"I want to practice getting my sex game right on you."

The moment the words left my lips, Jamal fell off his chair and hit the floor. In the process his glasses came off. He looked like a lost puppy, patting around trying to find them as he was blind without his glasses. I knelt down and picked them up. Before I handed Jamal his glasses, I stopped for a moment and stared at him. For the first time, I realized he was very cute. He had full, thick eyebrows that highlighted his light reddish skin. His profound jawline gave him an almost model look.

"Here you go." I put the glasses on Jamal's face.

He stood up straight, feeling mortified. He cleared his throat. "Thanks, Precious. Where were we?" he grabbed the book ignoring my proposition.

"We were talking about us, Jamal. Why won't you let me sex you up? I'm pretty sure you'll enjoy it."

"Sex me up...why me? You're the prettiest girl in our school, probably the prettiest girl I've ever seen. Any guy would want to be your first."

"For some reason I feel I can trust you. I don't believe you'll run around telling everybody we fucked. These clowns would make it their mission to let the whole hood know they popped my cherry. It's also very convenient because we live right next door to each other. Come on, Jamal. It'll be fun."

I folded my arms and began to tap my foot to let Jamal know I was pressed for time. I needed him to hurry up and get onboard with my plan. Any other boy in his position would already been trying to hump on me but Jamal clearly felt some kinda way. He probably figured he would remain a virgin until he was at least twenty-one and his first time would be with his wife. But if he was as smart with the girls as he was with the books, he would jump at this once in a lifetime opportunity. I mean how many boys were actually able to have sex with their first crush.

"Okay, I'll do it. When do you want to start practicing?"

"Right now, seems like the perfect time," I stated with a wide smile.

Refusing to give Jamal an opportunity to prolong this any further, I started to unbutton my jeans and pulled off my shirt. In a flash I was standing in my bra and panties. Jamal immediately got aroused. I grabbed the condom I had put in my jeans.

"We definitely not tryna make no babies up in here. Where do you want to do the deed at? A bed would be nice." I looked around the cramped bedroom

full of scientific posters and chemistry projects. I knocked a pile of books off the center of the bed. Jamal was still standing on the sidelines visibly petrified. Luckily, I had no problem taking the lead. After stripping him down to his underwear, I could see his dick trying to escape his boxer shorts. I was surprised that he was working with a nice-sized tool. When I reached to pull down his boxers, Jamal pushed my hand away.

"I can do that myself," he said meekly.

"I know you can. I'm just trying to help. I understand if you're a little nervous because I am too." That was a lie, but at this point I was willing to say anything to help Jamal relax. I was ready to get the deed done, which meant I needed Jamal's participation. "Come on, Jamal, we are almost there. Ain't no reason for you to be afraid."

I finally got Jamal to lay down on the bed, but he was still nervous. Without hesitation, I took off my bra and panties. My naked body had Jamal eyeing me like a dog in heat. I chose to straddle him. I heard that if you want to have control over a man you need to ride him. I definitely wanted to control Azar, so my pony game had to be tight. I planned to use my pussy as a weapon. I ripped open the condom package and slid it on Jamal's dick. I could feel his body shaking due his nervousness. It was a damn shame that the blind was leading the blind, but I had no doubt we would both be pros before long.

I lifted my ass on top and took the tip of Jamal's

dick and slowly let it play with the lips of my pussy. Then as I started getting wet, I led it to the center of my clit. Jamal was now making low moans as I let the head go in a little deeper. I wanted to take my time because, shit, I was a virgin, and I wanted to minimize the pain as much as possible. I then let another three inches slide inside of me and I let out a slight scream as he hit that spot.

Once I got over that initial hump, the next couple of inches weren't as bad and it started feeling good. It was feeling good to Jamal too, because his once low moans were reaching a much louder pitch. After about five minutes my wide hips began rocking in a seductive pace. I seemed like a natural. Before long I found myself able to twirl on his dick and riding him from the back. Right when I was fully in sync, Jamal let out a loud "Ahhhhhhh," as he bust a nut.

When I got up, Jamal took off his condom and noticed the slight traces of blood. He looked at me with a big grin and said, "You really were a virgin."

For the next week, every day after school Jamal and I got our sex on. As I predicted, we became pros. We even performed oral sex on one another, and he told me just how to suck it so I would have him cum within minutes.

With only a week left before the first of the mo-

nth, it was time to see if all my practice had paid off. With some money I had saved, I went and purchased a sexy outfit to wear to work. Although a bitch needed to hold on to her coins, I thought of this as an investment. Tomorrow, I would begin to implement my plan to lockdown Azar. I knew he had an afternoon appointment for a full-service detailing job, and I planned to look so luscious, he would have no choice but to believe I was the only girl for him.

Flawless

I woke up extra early in the morning to make sure my appearance was on point. I threw on a fresh fit I had ordered from one of those Instagram boutique stores. It was super cute and hugged my slim curvy body like second skin. I usually wore my hair in a long braid, but the night before, I put in a deep conditioner, and in the morning, I added some mousse, so my natural waves would hang smooth and free. "Lip gloss poppin', bitch, I'm showstoppin', Mwah." I blew myself a kiss and headed out the door.

When I pulled up to the car detailing shop, eyes followed me all the way inside. They were loving the way I walked, 'cause I was walking with a vengeance. You know how it be when you have a purpose. You put a wicked strut in each step.

Bree was behind the cash register, distracted counting money when I came in, so at first, she didn't

notice me enter.

"What's up, Bree!"

Bree nodded her head but didn't look up. While she continued to count money, I placed my purse on the counter near her. Which caught Bree's attention. She glanced at my purse and then her eyes traveled up taking in my entire glow up. She immediately stopped counting money and gave me that stare which screamed, bitch yes.

"Talk about a transformation. You look gorgeous," Bree beamed. I normally came to work in jeans or sweats, so my snatched ombre jumpsuit was giving off bad bitch vibes.

"You think so?"

"There's no think to it. It's a fact. I always told you how pretty you are but you're giving next level beautiful. Your options are about to be limitless when it comes to securing that baller you want."

"There is only one option I'm interested in, and his name is Azar."

"When Azar lays eyes on you, you'll have him on lock."

"That's the plan," I winked with a cunning smirk.

"Just remember to play your cards right and your plan will work." Bree closed the cash register and left the receptionist area. She headed to her office in the back, leaving me to keep my eye on the clock waiting for Azar to arrive for his scheduled appointment. While waiting for his arrival, a few different male customers came in flirting with me. I would politely smile but showed no interest. I was bored chewing gum and blowing bubbles until I saw Azar's clean cut fine ass enter the car detailing shop. I quickly took the gum out my mouth and threw it in the trash.

"Where's the usual girl at?" he asked, giving me a glimpse of his nice set of white teeth.

"Right here." I raised my right hand playing coy. "I'm the same girl."

Azar studied my face. I could tell he was trying to figure out what was different about me. "I decided to let my hair down, put on a little makeup...that's all."

"My fault. I need to start paying better attention to what's right in front of my eyes."

"Don't worry about it."

"Nah, I need to worry. To think all this time a pretty piece like you was right in front of me. That's a problem."

His fine ass had me blushing, playing with my hair and shit.

"What's your name anyway?"

"Precious."

"That's sexy, just like you. How 'bout we go and catch a movie and dinner? Say tonight if you not busy."

"I'd like that."

"Cool. What time you get off work?"

"Seven."

"A'ight. I'll be here then."

Azar paid for his service and exited the car de-

tailing shop leaving me with butterflies. A few minutes later, Bree entered from the back. I glanced around to make sure no customers were present before I put my excitement on full display. I started clapping my hands as if I won the come-up of the year award.

"Bree, Azar just asked me out and he's picking me up from work later on. You know I'm excited, but I need your advice about something."

"I told you. I knew once he saw you today, he would bite. So, what advice you need from me?"

"I can be straight up with you. I already told you I need money, and I need it quickly. So, how can I get Azar to spend his money on me?"

"When you dealing with these hustlers in the street, you just have to ask for what you want."

"Ask? Isn't that a little rude?"

"It's not what you ask; it's how you ask it. The same way a man is going to ask to get between your legs, the same way you ask him for whatever you want. But you want to politely present yourself as the prize. You'll be able to deal with any of these dudes out here but starting with Azar is a good look. He's getting money yet he low key."

"I agree. He checks all my boxes," I nodded.

"Understand something though, after whatever you have going on with him is over, you can only fuck with men that are equal or above him. That's how you keep your stock up. A lot of women pull themselves down because they start letting any piece of shit run up in them because they desperate for a dollar. No one is going to want to invest in that. It's not what you do but how you do it, so move wisely."

I took in Bree's advice and nodded my head with a knowing look. For the remainder of my work shift, I kept replaying the advice Bree gave me until I saw Azar pull up. He arrived at seven o'clock on the dot. I grabbed my purse, gave Bree a hug goodbye and headed out the door.

When I sat in Azar's car, I was in awe. I had never been in a Benz before. Even though I worked in a detailing shop and luxury cars were pulling in all the time, Bree never let me leave from behind the cashier desk. She stressed she needed my presence up front at all times.

So being in a luxury vehicle was new to me and now that I got a taste, this was the life I wanted. The way my ass melted in the seat when I got in his car. It was the softest leather I had ever felt in my life. Azar's Benz was a costumed white-on-white and his copper-toned complexion just glistened behind the wheel. We headed over the Brooklyn Bridge to the city. I rarely ever went to the city. It was like another world to me.

The night was crazy but in the best way. Azar was the first date I had ever been on, and he came correct. After the movie he took me to some fancy restaurant, and I even had wine. Nobody cared to card me. I didn't want the night to end.

When he pulled up in front of my apartment

building, at any moment I was expecting Azar to initiate sex, but to my surprise he didn't. He was the perfect gentleman. When I was about to get out the car, he grabbed my arm. "I wanna see you tomorrow."

"I'd like that."

"Good. What you wanna do?" I thought about his question for a second and decided to try my hand.

"I would love if you took me shopping. I wanna look good for you." There was complete silence, and I wasn't sure if Azar was going to push me out his car and speed off, offended by my suggestion. To my surprise he wasn't.

"I want you to look good for me, too. What time do you get off work tomorrow? I'll pick you up?"

"Actually, I have to go to school," I said wondering if he would start questioning my age.

"No problem, I'll pick you up from there."

"I'm in high school, Azar," I admitted, knowing he would eventually find out anyway.

"I figured that. Give me the time and address. I'll be there." After giving Azar the information, he kissed me on the cheek. I was grinning mad hard as I watched him drive off. I was stunned at how cool he was. Although I knew Azar was only nineteen, I wasn't sure how he was going to take dealing with a girl who literally just turned sixteen a few days ago.

The wide grin hadn't left my face as I put the key in the doorknob and entered the apartment. That was until a dirty, slight man, with emptiness in his eyes stumbled out the door. I stared him up and down then glanced over at my mother who was laying on the couch.

"Who was that?" I asked closing the door.

"Oh, he was just looking at your bedroom. He's a potential tenant."

"That won't be necessary, you'll get your damn money." I stormed off to my bedroom and slammed the door shut.

I was standing outside of school waiting for Azar to arrive. I was stoked about him taking me on a shopping spree today. In my head, I'd already picked out several outfits. Daydreaming about my runway looks, I was startled when Jamal walked up behind me and touched my shoulder.

"Where have you been, Precious? You haven't come over to study lately."

I rolled my eyes annoyed that I even had to explain myself to him. "I know, Jamal. Our studying is over. I learned everything I needed to."

"Just like that, it's over?" he hit me with this sad lost puppy glare, which had me confused.

"Jamal, it never started. I told you from jump that I needed your help to prepare me for this boy I was interested in. Well, now he's interested, so we done," I

snapped, walking off after seeing Azar pull up.

"Precious, wait!" Jamal grabbed my arm as I headed towards Azar's car.

"You betta get the fuck off me. Who you think you grabbing on?" I was burning a hole through Jamal. He was out of line putting his hands on me.

"Precious, I'm sorry. I didn't mean to grab your arm. I guess I miss you."

"Miss me?" I folded my arms and leaned back. "Jamal, we ain't in no relationship. It is what it is. We both got something out of it; now it's time to let it go. I'll see you around."

When I walked off, I knew Jamal was watching my every step. I greeted Azar with a smile when he got out and opened the passenger side door for me. I stared out the window and locked eyes with Jamal. He must have felt some kinda way when he saw me get in the car with Azar, but that wasn't my problem. He knew there were no strings attached. It wasn't my fault if he caught feelings. I brushed that shit off; Jamal was just a footnote in my past. As Azar drove away, I turned and gave him my attention because he was my present, and if things worked out, potentially part of my future.

Honeymoon Phase

After that day Azar took me shopping, for the next couple weeks, we were locked in, spending all our free time together. We went skating and riding on electric scooters through the Brooklyn Bridge Park. It was situated on the East River overlooking some of the best views of the Manhattan Skyline. He was constantly wining and dining me at his favorite eatery spots. Our relationship was coastin' like crazy on some *U My Everything*, we go together type shit, but yet we still hadn't fucked, and Azar didn't seem to be stressing it.

Before I knew it the first of the month had rolled around and I didn't have a dollar to my name. I knew I couldn't step up in my moms' crib without her money. My hands were sweaty as I built up the nerve to ask Azar for the cash. I kept thinking about what Bree said. It's not what you ask, it's how you ask.

Azar was dropping me off at home after we spent

another day together and we were talking while listening to music. He was leaned back in the driver's
seat, and I reached over, turning down the music.

"Azar, I need you to do me a huge favor."

"What is it, Ma?"

"My mother is stressin' me to give her money for
some bills. But I'm dead ass broke, and I was wondering if you could help me out?" I held my head down not
wanting to make eye contact with Azar.

"How much do you need?"

"A thousand."

"Don't ever be afraid to ask me for nothing." Azar
said reaching in his pocket pulling out a wad of cash.
I saw him counting out some money, then he put it in
my hand. "As long as you dealing wit' me, I got you."

Bree's advice proved to be golden, *it's not what
you ask, it's how you ask it,* I thought to myself while
counting the money Azar just gave me. I was ready to
do cartwheels down the hallway when I realized he
gave me an extra fifteen hundred dollars. I tried to
contain my excitement when I entered the apartment,
quietly locking the front door. As I tiptoed through the
living room, my mother flipped on the switch to the
lamp. The light seemed to be shining ultra-bright on
my moms, who was sitting on the couch holding an
open bottle of liquor in her hand.

"You got my money?" she asked like a raggedy
hoe.

"I need more time. I couldn't get it." I purposely

decided to fuck with my mother since she sounded so extra thirsty.

"I figured yo' silly ass wouldn't be able to come through. You been spending all that time wit' that boy and you can't even get no money outta him. I went in yo' closet and saw all those designer clothes he bought you. Most of it still got the tags on them. You betta take that shit back and get me my money."

"I can't do that. I don't have the receipts."

"Well then go pack yo' shit up and get the fuck out my house. Go stay wit' that boy you been fuckin'."

"You would really put your own daughter out on the street?"

"You damn right."

"You really are a no-good whore." I pulled out the money from my purse, tossing ten-hundred-dollar bills on the floor. "Pick that shit up like the crack whore you are."

My mother dropped to her knees and picked up the money without saying another word to me. I watched her with disgust before I went in my bedroom, locked the door and blasted my music. My mother was truly a simple-ass trick. For the first time, I had to admit to myself that I was ashamed to be her daughter.

Over the next several weeks, Azar and I continued

to get closer. I even started spending the night at his place and of course my mother didn't give a damn as long as I kept money in her pockets. One evening when I was staying at his apartment, I was laying on Azar's lap while we were watching a movie. I decided it was time for us to take our relationship to the next level and since Azar still hadn't tried, I made my move.

"Azar, do I look good to you?"

"Why you gonna ask me a dumb ass question like that. Do you think I would have you all up in my face if you didn't look good to me?"

"So why haven't you tried to have sex with me?"

"Because I can get sex from anybody. I'm not stressing it like that. I figured when you ready you'd let me know."

"Well, I'm ready."

"You sure? I ain't in no rush."

"I know. But you've been so good to me. I want to be good to you too."

I got up from the couch and quickly undressed, wanting to give Azar a clear visual of me wearing the super sexy lace bra and panty set that he bought me. I also wanted to showcase the skills I learned from fucking Jamal. Shit, I didn't want to feel like I put all that work in with Jamal for nothing. The lust in Azar's eyes told me I had played this just right.

First, I got down on my knees between Azar's legs. I unlatched his belt and unbuttoned his pants. He leaned his head back on the couch and closed his eyes, moaning in pleasure as I gave him the best blowjob this side of Brooklyn. I named myself the throat goat. His body jerked as I deep throated him. "Oh, Precious, just like that baby. Yeah, oh damn, baby," he said, moving the back of my head in a constant rhythm. I really fucked his mind up because not only did I let him come in my mouth, but I also swallowed. Then I rode his dick and when he screamed my name, I knew he was stuck. If I wanted him, he was all mine.

After our sex session, me and Azar officially became a couple, which meant he wanted to have me on lockdown. Since we started seeing each other, Azar would always drop me off and pick me up from work. Today he decided to get brand new. When he pulled up in front of the car detail shop, I was about to lean over and kiss him goodbye, but he stopped me.

"Tell Bree this is your last day." The confidence and boldness of Azar's statement made me pause for a second.

"Excuse me?"

"You heard me. I don't want you working there anymore."

"Why not?"

"I really shouldn't have to explain myself to you,

but since you're young, and this is new to you, I will. Too many maggots come through this shop, and I know they be after you. I keep a low profile. The last thing I need is for shit to get ugly due to one of these disrespectful niggas steppin' out of line, or because you do. Enough said, so tell Bree this your last day and I'll pick you up after work."

"Will do." I stated playing my position like a dutiful girlfriend.

I gave Azar a kiss goodbye, and that was it. He was right, though because I did begin scheming on getting two more just like him. With all the money he was now hitting me off with, if I had two other dudes to do the same, I would be sitting pretty as a pussy cat. I already paid my mother for four months in advance, plus I was ready to get the hell out that dump.

Azar suggested I move in with him, but I had no interest being on lockdown, so that was a no bueno. Of course, because of my age I couldn't get a crib, but Azar had a hookup with a building superintendent. At some point, I would start working on convincing him to secure an apartment for me.

"How did you like that restaurant?" Azar asked as we held hands walking towards his car.

"It was even more delicious than what you said.

That Jamaican curry and coco bread was some of the best I ever had."

"I told you ain't nothin' touching that Jamaican spot in Brooklyn. You betta listen to me when I speak!" he smiled, squeezing my hand. "Speakin' of listening to me, have you thought about what I asked you...moving in with me?"

Here we go again, I thought to myself. For the last couple weeks, I'd been pretending to consider Azar's idea about moving in with him, but I knew I needed to come up with a solid reason why that wouldn't work.

"I really want to, but my mother would probably try to have you locked up if I went that route." Being that my mother stayed high, she wouldn't give a fuck as long as I continued to hit her off each month, but my excuse sounded plausible.

Before Azar had a chance to respond we were interrupted because he got a call. Although he wasn't saying much, his facial expression showed signs of stress.

"Yep...I'm on the way," he said ending the call. "Change of plans. I need to make a stop right quick."

"Is everything okay? Your mood totally switched after that call."

"It will be, after I handle this," Azar said getting in the car.

"Handle what?"

"Don't worry about it. I got you."

Azar's blasé answer did not sit well with me. I

was looking for a more detailed explanation. Being a hood bitch and Azar being a hood nigga, I had felt we were the perfect match. But for the first time his energy was not meshing with mine. The mutual harmony was not there. I wanted to be wrong, but something wasn't right.

Never Be The Same

Azar pulled up to a building located in Brownsville, which was known for being the most dangerous neighborhood in New York. There were low-level drug dealers walking towards rundown buildings servicing the dope fiends who followed close behind. I noticed a group of teenagers playing loud trap music, smoking blunts, vapes and guzzling down liquor straight from the bottle, turning the block into their own nightclub. On the other side of the street there were a few women who were basically naked, twisting they ass past a group of men who were standing next to their luxury cars, in hopes one would bite and pay for some readily available pussy.

I continued glancing around taking in my surroundings. I peeped Azar reaching into a secret compartment in his car and grabbing his Glock. He placed it in the back of his pants before reaching for a second

gun and handing it to me. I was confused and nervous but didn't show it.

"Baby, you stay right here. Use this if need be. It's already loaded. Just pull the trigger. I'll be back in a minute."

I nodded my head and swallowed hard; doing my best to give the appearance I wasn't a novice at pulling the trigger. Once Azar was out of sight, I let out a heavy sigh. He left the engine running with the key fob in the center console. I stared down at the car fob and immediately locked the doors and clutched the Glock.

Although I grew up in the projects and had been walking through them all my life, for some reason waiting in Azar's car in the dead of night had my stomach in knots. Every other minute, I was staring out the window and double checking that the doors were locked. Being caught up in the unsavory scenery, I almost missed hearing the gunshots that were ringing in the smoke-filled air.

"Oh shit!" I screamed when I zeroed in on Azar hauling ass. From the one good light coming from the entrance of the building, I had a clear view of Azar running towards me carrying a big bag and aiming his Glock at a figure I couldn't see. Before I could even think, Azar was coming around to the driver's side and all I heard was what sounded like an explosion as the glass from the backseat window shattered.

"Open the fuckin' door!" Azar roared as he yanked the door latch back and forth. I forgot I locked the doors the minute he was out of sight. I fidgeted with the button because my nerves were shot. As soon as I heard the click of the doors unlock, I noticed the dude who shattered the backseat window getting closer to the car. He was just blasting out bullets on some terminator type shit. Still clutching the gun Azar gave me, I raised my arm out the window pulling the trigger in his direction letting off two shots, then I bent down to take cover. Azar tossed the black duffel bag in the backseat as I kept my head down and he sped off.

"Azar, what the fuck happened?" I sat up since we seemed to have escaped a bullet battle, but that didn't stop my hands from shaking. I was trying to remain as calm as possible but on the inside I was terrified. All it took was one bullet to end your life and that nigga who was chasing Azar had let out enough to kill a whole army.

I started interrogating him, but he remained on mute, keeping his eyes laser focused on the road while driving at a high speed. Even though Azar wasn't saying shit, all the sweat dripping down his face told me what I needed to know. It wasn't until after he pulled inside a parking garage and backed up the Benz next to his Range Rover to switch vehicles, did he seem to exhale. Azar quickly tossed a couple bags in the trunk. Once we were sitting in the Range, ready to exit, I figured he would spit out why we'd been caught up in a shootout, but I got nothing.

"Baby, can you please tell me what happened?"

Azar closed his eyes and put his head back. I figured that once again there would be a long stretch of silence, but instead he began to speak.

"The moment I knocked on the door I knew the vibe was off. But I couldn't walk away," he said with frustration in his voice.

"Walk away from what?" I asked, feeling like I was having to fight for an explanation as to why my life was put in jeopardy.

"A shady deal," Azar said shaking his head. "When I walked inside the apartment, the first thing one of the muthafuckas say to me was the heroin I sold them was trash. I knew that was straight bullshit because my connect is official. I brushed that shit off and was like okay cool just give me back my product. By this time, I had eyed the large black duffel bag against the wall, and I had a feeling my paper was in there."

"What did they say?"

"Nothing wit' their words, it was all wit' they eyes. I see the nigga standing closest to me wink his eye to the other nigga. I knew he was signaling for him to take me out. I had no choice but to pull out my gun and release them shots, 'cause it was either them or me. I dropped the nigga near me first. Once he was dead, I kept blasting. While the other nigga duckin' shots, I grabbed the black duffel bag and hauled ass."

"Yo, that shit is crazy. You was dealing wit' some serpents. What you gon' do now?" I asked, doubting Azar even knew.

"I can't go back to my crib—never. I'ma have to stay at a hotel until I come up wit' a better plan. Of course, you know I want you to stay wit' me."

"Azar, I...," I paused, hesitating for a moment. He must've sensed my reluctance because he unzipped the big black duffel bag, he had run out the building carrying. Azar took out five thousand dollars and put the money in my hand.

"This for being my gangster lil' Barbie."

I stared down at the five racks Azar put in my hand. The money quickly changed my mind. I looked back up at Azar. "I'm all in."

We basically locked ourselves in a hotel room for a couple days before stopping by my mother's apartment. I was only in there briefly but when I got back in the SUV, Azar seemed completely paranoid which made me feel anxious.

"Baby, is everything okay? You didn't see nobody did you?" I asked glancing out the passenger side window.

"Nah, I just don't like being nowhere around here."

"Well, you the one who wanted me to hide some of that money in my bedroom closet."

"I know, it ain't yo' fault. You've been a soldier

through all this." Azar reached over and took my hand. He gazed in my eyes for a second. "Honestly, Precious, I don't know what I would do without you. It's a major come up having you as my girl. I can feel that you're loyal. That means everything to me, especially with the business that I'm in. You the one fo'real."

"Like I said, I'm all in," I assured him. Azar kissed my hand and drove off.

After leaving my mother's apartment, Azar began to relax, no longer feeling we were being watched. So, we did a little shopping, went to the movies and had a nice romantic dinner. By the time we got back to the hotel, we were both exhausted and ready to chill.

"Fuck! I left that bag in the car!" Azar shouted as we were walking down the hallway towards our hotel room.

"We can get it later."

"No, it's the bag with the rest of my money I took from them snakes. Baby, I gotta shit bad as a ma'fuckah. Will you run down to the truck and get it?" he asked handing me the keys.

"Fine," I smacked annoyed as fuck. Last thing I felt like doing was going back to the car.

"Thanks babe," I heard Azar yell out as I made my way to the elevator.

When I finally got to the ground level, the garage was deserted. It was quiet to the point of being spooky. There was an uneasiness, as I glanced around. That eerie paranoia Azar had earlier today now had a chokehold on me. Once I spotted the truck, I sprinted towards it, popped the trunk, retrieving the bag and raced back to the elevator. I aggressively pushed the up button, wanting to hurry back to the hotel room. While waiting for the doors to open, I felt the cold tip of steel on the back of my head.

"Ain't this some shit," I blurted out. You know how you so scared you can't even be scared; that's how I felt. I knew that was a gun ready to blow the back of my brains out, but as bad as I wanted to cry, scream, or run, I was numb. I just thought to myself, *Is this it? Is this how I'm going to leave this world, brains splattered in the garage of a hotel?*

"I don't wanna kill you," I heard the baritone voice finally speak. "If you do what I ask, then you can walk away alive. The choice is yours."

"What's the choice?"

"All I want is the money and your boyfriend's life. If I don't get both, then I'm takin' yours."

"My boyfriend? Who my boyfriend?"

"Bitch, don't play wit' me. I saw you and Azar leave them projects hours ago and I been following you ever since. If I put my money on it, you the same girl that was wit' him when I blasted out his car window. What you gon' do, you ready to die or not?"

The gunman pressed the tip of his gun hard to

the back of my head causing it to jolt forward.

"So, you saying if I give you what you want you'll let me live?"

"I give you my word."

"Why you have to kill Azar though?" I asked, making a last-ditch effort to save Azar's life. "Isn't the money enough?"

"That was my brother he put a bullet in. He gotta die. Enough talkin'. What's it gonna be."

Without turning around, I handed the bag I just retrieved from the trunk to the gunman. I also handed him the key.

"Room 718."

Once I heard the gunman walking off, I turned quickly to get a glimpse of his face. I was able to catch a side profile. He had a distinguishable thick, razor edge scar going from the top of his cheek to the bottom of his chin. It was a disfigurement that I would never forget.

Elevate Your Life

4 Years Later...

It had been a little over four years since Azar's murder. During that time many things changed while some things remained the same. I went from living with my dope fiend mom in the projects, to lounging in my own crib with a Benz to match. The upgrade to my lifestyle was initially funded with the money Azar gave me to stash before his death. I continued to maintain it by dealing with niggas making money. I was a fast learner and quickly realized it was a mind game, and you gotta play this shit smart. Since none of the dudes I dealt with, I wanted to make my man, I kept it cool and didn't overstep my part. They served one purpose—to keep me paid and put up.

It was a hot summer day, and all eyes were on

me as I strolled down 125th and Lenox relishing in my ghetto fabulous dreams. When I reached the corner, while waiting for the light to turn, I stood in a 'I know I'm that bitch' position. That's when I noticed a guy who was fixated on me. He was trying to make his presence known by forcing us to make eye contact. I was used to niggas' mouths watering as they imagined how the insides of my pussy felt. With my low waist jeans perfectly accentuating the gap between my slightly curved legs and hourglass figure, the dude was in complete awe.

The closer he got to me, the more appealing I became. With the wind slightly blowing through my hair, the sun glistening on my skin putting my glow on ten and my glossy lips adding to my seductive appeal, I'm sure the nigga felt like he was supposed to have spotted me lounging by the beach on some exotic island instead of walking the grimy streets of Harlem.

"Excuse me, Ma, but can I speak to you for a moment, please?" he asked in his most sincere voice.

I folded my arms and stared at dude for a second. "I'm not yo' Ma. Save that shit for the next bitch," I smacked.

"Hold up a minute," he said grabbing my arm. Anger flashed from my eyes. "I'm sorry." He released his grip, placing both hands up. "I didn't mean to grab on you like that, but I didn't want you to walk away."

"Hum huh," I shot back rolling my eyes. "What the fuck do you want?"

"No disrespect, but you are far too gorgeous to be speaking with so much venom. The cursing isn't necessary. It's not a good look."

"Excuse me. Who the fuck is you? The Preacher's son?"

"Nah, my pops is dead, but when he was alive, he definitely wasn't a Preacher," he said with a devious chuckle.

"So why how I speak matter to you, since you ain't no savior?"

"I said my pops wasn't a Preacher. I didn't say I wasn't a savior."

"Lucky for me I don't need saving."

"I don't see a ring on your finger," he pointed out while caressing my left hand.

"Maybe I don't want a ring on my finger," I snapped pulling my hand away.

"All queens deserve to be blessed with the finest jewelry, including rings, and you're definitely a queen. If you don't mind, will you tell me your name?"

"Precious." I answered in a silky tone, which was in contrast to my once gritty voice.

"Your parents knew what was up when you were born, 'cause you damn sure precious."

"Cute, but I've heard all these lines before." Unimpressed, I gave him a nonchalant sigh.

Damn, he feeling himself, that shit sexy too, I thought to myself. After getting over my initial attitude, for the first time I actually swallowed the whole essence

of the man standing before me. His flawless mahogany skin was highlighted by a low cut with jet-black curls. He was six-foot-two and a solid one-ninety. His full lips were decorated with perfect white teeth. I had to admit he looked tasty like the finest piece of chocolate.

"So, what's your name?"

"Nico. Nico Carter."

"It's nice to meet you, Nico. Go 'head and shoot your shot. What you want from me?"

"Your company or maybe your hand in marriage, or maybe a pretty baby."

"I ain't making no baby for you."

"You say that now, but just give me a month. When I elevate your life, you'll be begging to have my seed."

"You real cocky wit' yours." I gave him a confused stare. "What you pushin'?"

"What you mean what I'm pushin'?"

"You know what I mean. What type of foreign you got?"

"Oh, you mean car. Precious, that's not the type of question you ask a man when you just meet him. He might get the wrong impression and assume you a paper chaser," he added. I had to stop myself from laughing in his face.

"Bro, you got me confused with the next bitch. I don't give a fuck what impression I give off. I don't fuck wit' broke niggas. A broke nigga make for a dry pussy. Men makin' money sponsor goals. You feel me?"

I said that shit extra slow to make sure he received the message.

I knew every instinct in Nico's body was telling him to walk away and never look back at the danger standing before him, but being a typical nigga with a hard-on, his lust prevailed.

"I tell you what, let me take you on a date tonight, and I promise you won't be disappointed."

Nico handed me his phone. I put in my contact information while giving him a lingering smile.

"You definitely gonna be my permanent piece," he nodded with the utmost confidence.

I figured that instead of turning Nico off with my slick-with-the-mouth antics, I was pulling him further in. He probably wasn't used to my type, a woman so blatant with it. He had to respect the fact that I let it be known that you either step up or shut up.

After my encounter with Nico, I went to the Dominican spot for my bi-weekly wash and blow out. I was under the steamer with deep conditioner in my hair replying to his text messages, smiling the entire time. He wanted confirmation that I wasn't going to renege on our date tonight. He didn't need to know it, but I was actually looking forward to it. While enthralled in reading his latest text, I was rattled by someone

pounding on the steamer. Once I realized it was my bestie Inga, I got excited.

"What up baby girl!" Inga had a huge smile on her face.

"Bitch, you was 'bout to catch these hands," I laughed, lifting up the hood so I could hear what Inga was saying. "I was like who the fuck bangin' on this steamer like a crazy person. I should've known it was yo' silly ass."

We both laughed as Inga sat down in the empty chair next to me.

"So, what's up wit' you tonight, we going to the hookah bar?"

"Actually, I have a date."

"A date?" Inga leaned in close and gave me this *I need all the details* stare. "Who you fuckin' wit'?"

"I ain't fuckin' wit' nobody. I just met this guy on my way over here, and we supposed to link up tonight."

"Is that who you was texting when I came in and had you smiling and shit?" she teased.

"Yeah, he was confirming we were still on for tonight."

"He got money?" Inga questioned rubbing her fingers together.

"I hope so, but if not, the date will end before it even starts. If he don't pull up in some official shit, I won't have no problem telling him to forget my name and number."

"Exactly. That dick don't come wit' some money,

you can't lay wit' it. It's not a game out here. But if he do got that paper, you know you have to hook me up with one of his friends. Men wit' money usually move wit' a crew."

"If he legit, I'll hook you up wit' one of his friends so we can both get paid. You know I got you." We nodded our heads in agreement, linking our index finger together.

And I would always have Inga's back. We had been close since sixth grade, but in the last couple years we became even closer. When I moved out my moms' crib and changed schools, I missed having a female friend. All the girls at my new high school had established their cliques and looked at me as an outsider and unwanted competition. It didn't help that I was the 'it' girl all they boyfriends was lusting after. I would vent to Inga, so she would come over and spend just about every weekend with me to make sure I wasn't lonely. Plus, we both preferred dealing with hustlers, which kept us going on double dates. Once we graduated from high school, we became twins, doing everything together.

"I know you do, just make sure he ain't no lame nigga. I hope he's a keeper," Inga winked. "Now let me leave, so you can get dolled up for your date tonight. We'll talk later," she said before we exchanged air kisses. I couldn't help but grin as I watched Inga strut out the beauty salon, as I too hoped she was right, and Nico would be a keeper.

A Dream Simple Fantasy

When I stepped out the entrance of my apartment building on Riverside Drive, my eyes lit up when Nico was standing in front of his matte mystic blue AMG G63. I was on full beam as he held the passenger door open for me.

"By that smile on your face, I'm assuming this is Precious approved."

"Is it that obvious?" I giggled as Nico closed the door and got in on the driver's side.

"So where do you want to go tonight?"

"Maybe dinner."

"You got a place in mind?"

"It doesn't matter. As long as we're together." I stated sweetly. He might prove to be cuff material, so I was making sure to have my charm oozing.

"Good answer," Nico looked over at me and said, before pulling off.

"I know I already told you this but thank you for dinner. I've never been to a restaurant in Soho before. It was different but nice," I said as we took a nighttime stroll through Riverside Park. Nico raised his arm towards me, and I gladly slid my fingers through his hand.

"Yeah, I've learned that sometimes different can be good."

"What else have you learned?"

"Learned..." Nico raised an eyebrow.

"Yes. I guess what I'm really asking is for you to tell me about yourself. You know, growing up, life experiences. Things that you learned along the way and had a major impact on your life."

He paused for a moment, seeming to be in deep thought. "I was always told childhood trauma triggers everything. With that said, the biggest impact for me was my father getting murdered. I was thirteen at the time but some days that hurt is fresh as if it happened yesterday."

"Murdered...what happened?"

"He was in the streets. Opps took him out. He used to hustle with my best friend Ritchie's dad. We

grew up in the same projects and our mothers were best friends. Shortly after my dad got killed, Ritchie's dad got locked up on some federal charges. He's doing life. With both of them gone, I had to step up and hold everything down."

"That's a lot to take on at thirteen."

"It's a cold world. In the streets it's kill or be killed. Age don't matter. What mattered to me was following in my father's footsteps but staying alive in the process. One of the men that worked for my dad's organization, took me under his wings. Taught me the drug game. Eventually I brought Ritchie into the fold. We made a pact to never leave one another's side, until death do us part." Nico stopped mid step and put his head down.

"Is something wrong?" I asked when there was a lengthy period of silence.

"I'm shocked I just told you all that. I don't typically open up like this. But that's okay because you gon' be my girl. I know it."

"Why you so pressed for me to be your girl?" I was curious to know. Nico embodied the three "c's" cute, confident, and charismatic, plus the nigga seemed to have his paper straight. Which meant pussy was thrown at him on a daily. I needed an understanding what his fascination with me was.

"Besides the fact that you are unbelievably gorgeous, something about you is dark."

"Dark? What the fuck?"

Nico gave me that look. "I told you earlier about your mouth. You much too pretty for such abrasive talk."

"I meant to say, please explain what you mean." *This cussing situation was definitely gonna be a problem,* I thought to myself.

"That same look I got in my eyes, you got it in yours. I've never met a woman or man besides my father with that look."

"What look is that?"

"It's a combination of many things. The average nigga wouldn't be able to handle you, but I know I can and will. Besides, you already mine."

"I'm starting to think you might be right."

"Of course I am, I'm always right." Nico boasted, giving me a devilish smile.

With the majority of niggas I fucked with, I wouldn't give them no ass until after they had tricked several stacks on me, but not with Nico. I willingly gave up the pussy that first night. It was crazy because no matter how hard I tried; he wouldn't let me get on top. That let me know he was determined to maintain control over me and our relationship. But with his incomparable fuck skills, I didn't have a problem with it. From that day on it was like that Biggie classic, *Just Me and My Bitch.*

Being Nico's girl was like being the First Lady. The streets made him their king, so they bowed down to me as if I was their queen. I had to take it back to Brooklyn on a regular basis and represent my hood. See, Harlem wasn't my hood, I rep'd for BK. The first time I drove up to Bree's car detailing spot in Nico's matte blue G-Wagon, the place paused. They knew it was Nico's shit, and I had to be his girl to be pushing his whip. For everyone else who didn't know, there was no doubt in their mind I was some powerful ma'fucka's wifey.

I loved the stares and glares I received from dealing with a kingpin. Even for the people who hated on me, they didn't have the balls to say anything to my face. Nico's reputation preceded him, and no one crossed him, and since I seemed to be the closest thing to him, they didn't dare cross me either.

I was admiring my reflection in the bathroom mirror at Nico's Brooklyn Heights Brownstone, putting on some lip gloss and reminiscing on how I got here, cuffed to this man. Not that I was complaining. It was just Nico had us on autopilot. Overnight he went from excuse me miss to we got life together. The next morning after we had mind blowing sex, he said I was moving in with him. He didn't ask, he demanded. He was so cocky, confident, and controlling with his shit, but it turned me on. He officially had my head fucked up. In the midst of daydreaming, I heard the doorbell ring. I stopped what I was doing to see who was at the door. Because the same way Nico wanted to dominate me, I was territorial over him.

I stopped and listened intently when I saw Ritchie and Tommy in the foyer discussing business with Nico.

"How things going with that new zone we supplying?" Nico asked Tommy.

"So far, business is good. Actually, better than good." Tommy gave a humble brag. "I can give you a more accurate profit amount when I get back to the warehouse," he added.

"That's what I like to hear. I expect you to hit me later with those numbers," Nico told him, keeping his tone subtle. That was one of the traits I admired about him. Nico had this way of politely demanding shit, which in turn made you want to please him even if it was an inconvenience.

"You got it boss."

"Tommy, I'll be by the warehouse later to check on things. Don't let none of the workers leave until I get there," Ritchie demanded, fake poking out his chest like he ran shit. I frowned listening to Ritchie insert his two cents when nobody asked for it but that was his typical behavior.

By the way Tommy brushed him off, he too knew Ritchie was only trying to show some authority. Nico and Tommy did a quick dap before he nodded bye to

Ritchie and left out. Ritchie's frustration due to Tommy's dismissive attitude was evident. Because although Ritchie was Nico's right-hand man, he didn't garner the same level of respect as Nico. The whole borough knew that Nico basically handed large portions of the business over to his best friend out of loyalty, not because Ritchie earned it, of course Nico didn't see it that way. As far as he was concerned, he and Ritchie were brothers.

"Man, you too lax wit' these niggas. They be coming at you like ya friends instead of your workers," Ritchie whined.

"Nah, it's not like that. They know who's boss, but I prefer for them to feel comfortable around me."

"Comfortable?! Fuck that, you better make them goofy niggas fear you," Ritchie spit with agitation.

"My temper is legendary, so they all know what it is. Our crew are the eyes and ears of the streets. They gotta believe they can tell me anything. Without information I'm powerless. So, I don't need them to fear me, fear brings about lies," Nico explained maintaining his cool.

"I hear you, but sometimes you need to keep your foot on they neck as a reminder," Ritchie stressed.

As I listened to them exchange words, I knew that Ritchie didn't understand that Nico had a different style of dictatorship. Ritchie being partial to establishing an atmosphere of tyranny actually worked well for many bosses in Nico's position, but Nico vehemently opted against it. See, Nico wasn't big on bluffing. If he had to instill fear in you, that meant your time was up, and your life was over. He maintained a calm, cool and collected persona that made even his worse enemies respect him. When the dark side of Nico appeared, everyone knew to stay away.

"I'll think about what you said," Nico answered, trying to get off the subject.

Right when Nico got his last word out, Ritchie noticed me entering the foyer. Nico followed Ritchie's gaze, and both of their eyes were on me.

"What's up, Precious?"

"The same thing, Ritchie," I replied dryly.

"When you gonna hook me up wit' one of your girls?"

"The only girl I fuck wit' is Inga, and I already gave you her number."

"Well, set up a date for us."

I let out a heavy sigh not in the mood to entertain Ritchie's antics. "Every time you tell me to do that shit you always cancel at the last minute."

"I tell you what, we can do some double date type shit. There's this new lounge I've been wanting to hit up anyway."

Ritchie directed his attention to Nico, nodding his head to get him to agree.

"Why we gotta come?" I asked wanting to shut the idea down before Nico gave it consideration.

"It'll be fun. Let's do it tonight. Right, Nico."

Ritchie playfully punched Nico's shoulder, pushing him to cosign.

"Yeah, it'll be cool," Nico agreed.

"Fine, but you call Inga and let her know, so if you cancel, it's all on you."

"I won't be cancelling," Ritchie insisted, turning to Nico. "You ready?"

"Give me a second. I'll meet you outside."

Ritchie stalled for a moment, like he wanted to stay. Finally, he exited out the front door and Nico walked in my direction. He stood behind me, lifting my hair, sprinkling soft kisses on my neck. My eyes closed, craving more. Being with him was a dream a simple fantasy yet my reality.

"I have to step out for a few hours, to handle some business with Ritchie. I'll be back later, so we can link up with him and Inga."

"I miss you already." I turned to face Nico wanting to feel the softness of his kisses on my lips.

"I'll see you when I get back."

I kissed Nico one last time, slowly releasing his hand not wanting him to slip away from me.

Triggering Thoughts

When we arrived at the upscale lounge, I was impressed with the chic antique ambiance. There was exposed handmade brick, extended polished wood bar, vaulted ceilings with massive crystal chandeliers, and wood panel artwork. The decor in combination with the plush sofas and soft lighting gave you swank hotel lobby vibes, putting you at ease. So, at ease that by the time we got to the area where Ritchie and Inga were settled in, you would've thought they were sitting on a bed instead of a couch. Once realizing we arrived, they stopped themselves from damn near having sex on the sofa.

"What up man!" Ritchie smiled pulling a bottle of champagne from the ice bucket, but it was empty. He then opened another bottle and filled up me and Nico's glasses.

"Hey Precious," Inga giggled in that tipsy, I'm

ready to fuck voice.

"I see you lit over there," I said sitting down next to Nico. He put his arm around me and made small talk with Ritchie. I continued to sit back holding my glass of champagne observing Ritchie and Inga's interaction. When Ritchie turned to refill her glass, Inga seemed lost in his gaze. She was hanging on to his every word like a lovesick schoolgirl. She was wearing this short dress, giving Ritchie easy access to squeeze her thighs and grope her. At one point, his hand was damn near inside Inga's coochie. She was giggling, while he whispered in her ear. Right when I was about to tell them to get a room, Ritchie said they was leaving. I gave Inga a hug goodbye and she hurried off reaching for Ritchie's hand.

"I had a good time tonight," Nico said as he drove us home. "We should all hang out more often. Next time do dinner."

"Baby, do you really think we should be making future dinner dates with those two? I mean how long can their relationship actually last?"

"Ritchie seemed like he was really feeling her."

"Yeah, feeling up her ass."

"Stop it. I'm just saying they seem to enjoy one another. It's cool. Inga's your best friend and Ritchie's mine. We have a nice little family thing going on."

I secretly hoped that Ritchie was so bad in bed Inga would promptly cut him off and beg me not to remind her she ever let him sniff her panties. As far as

I was concerned, Ritchie was not only a lame nigga but a menace, and I didn't want him in no family of mine.

"Let me ask you something, Nico."

"Go right ahead."

"You don't ever feel like Ritchie just riding yo' dick and not bringing nothing to the table? He always wants to regulate some shit and scold you on how to handle your business, but it's all dead noise. That shit don't bother you, 'cause it irks my nerves."

"Precious, you too hard on Ritchie. Sometimes he has to throw his weight around a little bit in order to feel like a man, but it's harmless. He might have his faults, but the reason why I keep him by my side is because he's loyal. With the game I'm in, that's a character flaw. These niggas out here ain't got no loyalty to nobody, but Ritchie got my front and my back." Then Nico turned and looked at me with a smirk on his face and said, "Listen here. I'm like a dog, I don't speak, but I understand everything. Ritchie is good people, trust me."

I sat there in the passenger seat, just nodding my head. The conversation was a lost cause. Nico was dead set on his opinion of Ritchie, which was disappointing to me. I always viewed Nico as a dude that was beyond reproach when it came to his street savvy. But if he honestly believed that Ritchie was loyal, then he had the game all fucked up.

The next day, early in the afternoon, as if reading my mind, Inga called me while I was in the kitchen pouring myself something to drink before heading out.

"What's going on, Inga."

"Girl, Ritchie can fuck! He just left here like an hour ago!" Inga sounded as if she was on her honeymoon and had been freshly dicked down.

"Where was yo' moms at when all that fucking was jumpin' off?"

"She went to Philly this weekend to visit her sister, so I had the place to myself. Girl, I'm in love wit' that nigga!"

"Whateva, Inga. You say that about every dude that beats that coochie good."

"This time was different. He was so gentle with me and before he left, he gave me a band and told me to get my hair and nails done."

"Ritchie might have potential." I stated feeling optimistic for my girl. I had to admit, I was surprised by what Inga was telling me. I always thought of Ritchie as being a five-minute fuck. I definitely didn't think he would lay up with a bitch or leave her money to get her nails and hair done. "You deserve a man to pamper you."

"Right! I do deserve a man to assist with my glow up. Girl, if he spoils me the way Nico do you, I promise I'll suck his dick every morning when he wakes up and every night before he go to bed."

"Bitch, you stupid. I'm happy for you though. But don't get too caught up in Ritchie. I would hate for him to get you open, then break your heart."

"I got this. But let me go. I can't be late for my hair and nail appointment. I want to be extra cute for my date with Ritchie tonight. Bye."

I couldn't help but smile after my call with Inga. It was nice hearing my bestie sounding all extra giddy. Not only that, but they were also going on a second date already. Maybe Ritchie wasn't as bad as I thought, and I needed to delete him from my shit list. Because if Inga was happy, then so be it. She deserved for a nigga to upgrade her. I decided to call Nico and find out if he'd gotten any feedback from Ritchie. Inga was my girl, and I would feel some kinda way if he played her out. My call went straight to voicemail.

Nico's phone was doing that a lot lately. For a second, I wondered if the nigga was creeping on me with the next bitch but decided I was being paranoid. Not saying that Nico wasn't capable of cheating like any other man, but Nico knew he would have to be extra discreet with his shit. I don't play about no side bitch; I made that clear about a hunnid times. My motto was always, I don't trust these niggas, so don't put your trust in me but I allowed myself to think different when it came to my relationship with Nico.

I stared at the picture of us on my iPhone's lock screen. "If Nico is fucking around on me, it better be when he's going in and out of town."

Seek & Destroy

I had not seen my mother in months, so I decided to stop by and check on her before I went to get my car detailed at Bree's shop. Even though I didn't fuck with her like that, I wanted to make sure she hadn't died of a drug overdose. I used my key, and when I opened the door, my mother was lying on the couch, butt ass naked with some dude on top of her. Empty bottles of liquor were scattered around the couch and some needles and pipes were sitting on the table next to them. They were motionless and for a second, I thought they were dead until I heard moaning. I walked over to the old stereo system and blasted the music to wake the two junkies up. They jumped off the couch in panic mode like someone smoked up their last hit.

"What the fuck is going on! Who the hell is you?" he sounded groggy as fuck.

I turned down the music. "I'm her daughter. Can

you leave because I need to speak to my mother...
alone."

"We can talk later. It's too early in the morning
for this shit," my mother mumbled.

"It's the middle of the afternoon. The morning
been over," I informed them, then pointing my finger
at the clothes on the floor. "Now, my man, get dressed
and get the fuck outta here 'cause I need to speak to
my mom."

The man looked over at my mother, as if waiting
for her to speak up on his behalf but she turned her
face away and ignored him. I folded my arms, eyeing
him harshly. "Can you please hurry the fuck up."

The man was mean mugging me the entire time
as he moved in slow motion to get dressed. When he
picked up his keys from the table, he reached for the
small amount of drugs left over from their all-night
bender.

"I paid for this. Get yo' hands off my shit!" My
mother snapped, smacking his hand.

"Listen, we ain't 'bout to have no crackhead fight
up in here. Take that shit Pookie and get the fuck out."

"My name ain't Pookie. It's Leroy."

"Whatever, just go."

I followed the man to the door and locked it to
make sure he didn't try to get back in on some sneak
shit. I headed back into the living room to have a come
to Jesus moment with my mother. I realized she had
disappeared into the bathroom when I heard the door

slam. I was willing to wait it out and although she was trying my patience, eventually she walked back into the living room smoking a cigarette.

"You grown and can do whatever you like, but not on my dime. You're bringing any ole type of dusty nigga in here fuckin' them wit' no condom or nothin'. Are you tryna die?"

"Just because you give me money, I'm still yo' mother, and you don't tell me what to do."

"How 'bout I don't give you any more money, and you do whatever the fuck you like."

"Precious, you know I need that money to survive."

"Then act like it. Keep them lowdown niggas outta here. They might flip out and kill yo' ass. I know one day I'm gonna have to bury you, but I would hate for it to be over some shit like that."

My mother decided to mosey along to the table and pick up an open bottle of beer, taking a long gulp. "Are you done lecturing me?" she asked after finishing it off.

I unzipped my purse, pulling out some money when it became evident my mother was not about to undergo that difficult but powerful realization she had to change her behavior.

"I know you'll probably smoke this up in less than a week, but I'll never stop praying that one day you'll decide to get clean. If so, I'll gladly pay for you to check into a rehab facility."

I placed the money in my mother's hand and held it tightly for a second staring into her eyes. I was trying to reach her soul, but it was way past time I accepted it would never happen.

After I left my mother's apartment, I sat in the car staring at my reflection through the rearview mirror. Our encounter left me emotionally drained. I called Nico figuring hearing his voice would take the edge off and put me at ease.

"Straight to voicemail again? What tha fuck!" I fumed, hitting the end button and tossing my phone on the passenger seat before I sped off.

I headed straight to the detail shop in search of some much-needed relationship guidance. As I was getting out my car, I saw Bree speaking with a customer. I practically jumped across the parking lot to reach her.

"Excuse me, I need to borrow Bree for a minute," I said interrupting their conversation.

"Give me a moment," she told the customer.

"Bree, sorry for interrupting you, but this is an emergency. I'm sure the look of stress is written all over my face."

Bree stopped me on our way to the entrance of the car detailing shop and took a moment to size

me up. I was giving rich bitch street glam, but it was camouflaging my inner turmoil.

"Nah, I don't see stress. You looking like new money to me."

When we entered Bree's office, she sat down in the chair behind her desk in business mode. I slumped down on the couch, exhaling loudly like I had been carrying a heavy load.

"I might appear to have it all together on the outside, but on the inside I'm just tryna maintain."

"From what I hear you're more than maintaining. I hear Nico is taking real good care of you. The streets say you all live like rap royalty."

"Oh, that's what the streets say? They saying anything else?"

"Anything else like what?"

"You know, what bitch is fuckin' my man."

"Precious, I know you not feeding into silly shit like that." Bree leaned forward, crossing her arms on her desk. "Your only concern should be that Nico show you respect. What you think the streets might be saying is irrelevant."

"What's irrelevant about wanting to know if my man is fucking around on me?"

"Because you don't need to stress over something you have no control over."

"Is that what you said about Clay before he got locked up? You were never stressed about the next bitch?"

"Fuck no. For what? I can't control that man's dick. I minded my business and believed he would always do right by me. And guess what, he did. When he got locked up, he gave me the house, cars, this detailing shop and whatever money was left over after lawyer fees. Enjoy the life Nico is providing for you. If you start looking for dirt on him, you'll find it. Don't bring unnecessary drama into your life."

"I hear you, Bree. You know I always appreciate your advice. I'm going to mind my business. Unless some shit about Nico and another bitch slaps me in the face, this is a dead issue for me," I vowed.

I was sipping on a glass of wine, admiring my fresh pedicure waiting for Inga to arrive. We were having lunch at this swanky restaurant in the city that Nico had taken me to a few months ago. I hadn't seen my girl in a minute and with the weather being so nice, I thought this was the perfect spot for us to sit outside, have a good meal and of course some drinks.

My appetite was starting to get the best of me, but right before I was about to text Inga and ask her what was taking her so long, she popped up.

"Girl, look at you!" I stood up and gasped. We hugged each other for a few seconds, then Inga stepped back and did a few cute poses showing off her glow up.

"I'm spending Ritchie's money nicely, huh?" she winked her eye and sat down at the table.

"Damn right. I don't see you for a few weeks and you show up looking like a snack. Love the outfit and haircut," I said admiring the taupe tube top with lace trim and the matching high waisted flare pants.

"Yeah, being with Ritchie, he makes me wanna be very demure, very mindful, very cutesy, plus I got tired of him pulling on my lace front wigs while we be fucking, so I decided to rock my own hair and got what I call a very demure bob." Inga smiled widely shaking her blunt chin length cut.

"Well, I don't know about none of that demure shit but bitch you ate. I'm impressed."

"I can't lie, it feels nice having a man spoil me," Inga acknowledged as she eyed the waitress who placed a drink in front of her.

"I know what you like so I went ahead and ordered that for you," I informed Inga.

"Good looking out," she nodded, immediately taking several sips. "But yeah, Ritchie is everything to me. I can't imagine my life without him. Let me stop. I keep rambling on about me and Ritchie. How are you and Nico doing?"

"Me and Nico are cool, I guess," shrugging my shoulders as we glanced over the menu. Inga stopped looking at food options and rested her eyes on me.

"What you mean you guess? Ya the King and Queen of the streets. You should be on top of the world."

"I suppose but between you and me, I think Nico out here cheating. I know most niggas get they shit off, but I don't think this no he bust a nut and that's the end of discussion type shit."

"Why you say that?"

"Just a feeling, but I could be wrong."

I noticed Inga fidgeting in her chair. It was obvious from her body language she was hiding something.

"Inga, do you have info you should share, 'cause you my girl? If you know something, spit it out."

"I didn't wanna say nothin' because I thought it was just some hatin' shit by jealous hoes. But last week I ran into Tanisha. She told me she heard Nico was fuckin' wit' this chick named Porsha from Queens."

"How did she hear about it?"

"Tanisha said her cousin Michelle is good friends with the girl Porsha. She was bragging about how she was fuckin' wit' Nico Carter. She said she knew he had a girl but didn't care 'cause he had some good dick and kept her pockets heavy. Even if it's true, forget about her. You know these chicks dying to walk in your shoes, but you're Nico's main girl, not them."

I'm supposed to be his only girl, I fumed on the inside as I took in what Inga told me. I leaned back in the chair, cradling my glass of wine, trying to keep my composure. I kept my gaze on her but remained silent. I had no intentions of letting my best friend know that at this very moment I had begun plotting how I would teach Nico the ultimate lesson for betraying me.

Major Moves

For the next couple of weeks, every day and every night I thought about the information Inga gave me. As bad as I wanted to put a knife through Nico's heart, I remained silent. I was spending each moment trying to figure out how to cause him the type of pain where he would wish he was dead, but he was very much alive. It was difficult though, because I couldn't just dump him and be with the next nigga; the code of the streets wouldn't allow that. The only dude I would want was someone on Nico's level, and all kingpin's wifey and ex-wifey were off limits. I also wanted to make sure my paper was intact before I bounced. There were so many things to think about. But the one thing I was sure of—a nigga was not gonna play me. That meant Nico had to go.

"Girl, I'm so glad you said we should go to the club and have some fun tonight. I needed this," I admitted, as we sipped champagne in the VIP section.

"I figured you did. Plus, with Nico and Ritchie out of town, it was perfect timing. It feels like the old days when we were out here running the streets like single sluts."

"Biiiiitch!" we laughed so hard I almost spit out my champagne. But Inga was right, being tipsy, shaking my ass to music was the perfect antidote to get my mind off Nico. But my fun was cut short. Right when I grabbed the champagne bottle to refill my glass, I spotted three women coming towards our booth. I only recognized one, which was Tanisha.

"What's up, Precious, Inga," Tanisha greeted us in a dry ass voice. Me and Inga nodded our heads to acknowledge her. "This my cousin Michelle and her friend Porsha."

Inga and I sneaked a peek at each other then I locked eyes with Porsha. I was mindin' my business, these bitches mindin' me. Tanisha introducing me to the hoe who was fucking my man had me bitter and ready for war. Typically, I ain't fightin' no random but I was about to make an exception. As I considered if I should lay hands, I couldn't help but stare down who I somewhat considered my competition.

Technically, she wasn't competition because I was the one that represented as wifey. However, because I was competitive by nature, I had to size her up that

way. The girl was attractive and had a nice body too. We somewhat shared a slight resemblance; except she was more hard-core looking in the face. I didn't know if it was due to age or just living a hard knock life.

"Tanisha, since yo' goofy ass wanted to bring your people over here, let's get right to it. Porsha, are you fuckin' my man, Nico?"

"Excuse me?"

"You bird bitch, you heard me. You fuckin' my man, Nico or what?"

Porsha placed one hand on her hip, and waved her other hand in my direction, while twisting her neck and doing the most. "As a matter of fact, I am, bitch!" Porsha announced loudly, being extra bold.

Inga, Tanisha and Michelle stood frozen waiting to hear my response, but for now, fuck talking. This trick was begging to catch these hands. I wanted to beat the taste out her mouth. I went full blown ratchet on this hoe. As if GloRilla knew what was about to go down, her song TGIF was blasting in the back.

Friday night, hot as hell, and you know the hoes out
Mani', pedi', fresh set, and I got my toes out
I'm rocking off-white on an off night
These bitches with me pretty, and they all can fight.
I'm looking fine as hell, I'm tryna be seen
I'm finna wreck the scene...

I clutched the champagne bottle tighter, with the intent on putting that muthatfucka to work. I stood on top of the booth and jumped across the table, swinging the bottle at Porsha. Michelle snapped out of her daze right when the bottle was about to collide with Porsha's head and knocked it out my hand. It didn't matter because I had two good fists that would finish the job for me. I threw my whole body on top of Porsha. She was petite so she went down like a thin piece of paper. I just kept swinging on the bitch. A right and a left then another right and another left.

The bitch was helpless. Right when Michelle was about to jump on my back, Inga stepped up and let her know to back the fuck up. This won't no tag team shit. Everybody knew Inga could fight. But the funny thing was, because of how I looked, the whole hood slept on me, but I was 'bout it. Although with Porsha I was boxing a featherweight.

Inga was probably the only person that knew I could fight my ass off, and that's only because I had to lay hands on her one time. I kept throwing the punches, then I took my shoe off and clobbered the bitch with my heel. Right when I started seeing blood, security ran up and lifted me off the bruised and bloody hussy.

"Now go tell Nico I dragged yo' ass, bitch!" I taunted before I spit on her.

The next day I slept until the middle of the afternoon. I couldn't stop the dreams of beating the shit out of Porsha. Right when I was about to take my knife and slit her throat, I felt someone touching my shoulder and saying my name.

"Precious, Precious." I shrugged my arm, but the touching persisted. When I opened my eyes, it was Nico.

"Baby, are you OK?" I turned my head, pissed he interrupted me right before I was about to end Porsha's life. "I came home as soon as I heard what happened."

"I'm fine. You need to go check on yo' bitch."

"Precious, what are you talking about?" he was calm and sane to gaslight me into believing I was the crazy one.

"Don't play wit' me, Nico. I know all about you and Porsha. That's why yo' phone always be going to voicemail 'cause you laying up wit' that hoe. Fuck you and that bitch!"

I pulled my favorite ultra soft cashmere throw blanket over my head to go back to sleep. I wanted a moment to put Nico and his side chick out my mind. But instead of giving me space, he grabbed my blanket and threw it on the floor.

"I told you about that slick ass mouth of yours!" he raged pointing his finger in my face.

I rose up in the bed like I was possessed. "I don't give a fuck if you like what's comin' out my mouth or not. You runnin' round here fuckin' that cunt, and then the dumb bitch wanna step to me at the club. You lucky I didn't kill that hoe!"

"Precious, I'm not fuckin' that girl. Whatever she told you was a lie."

"You must think you dealing wit' a straight dummy. I ain't no goofy bitch. How did you find out about the fight?"

"Inga called Ritchie and told him. Then he told me." Nico stated after a long pause.

I nodded my head, getting out of bed to retrieve my phone off the dresser. I could feel Nico's eyes following me.

"Who you calling?"

"Inga. I'ma ask her if she called Ritchie and told him what happened."

Nico grabbed the phone out of my hand. "What the fuck you need to call Inga for? There's no reason to get her in the middle of our shit."

"Muthafucka, you put her in the middle. You know damn well you didn't find out from Ritchie. The bitch you fuckin' came whining to you. I'm done. Go be wit' her, 'cause I won't have no problem replacing you."

I threw my hand up and turned to walk away from Nico when he grabbed me by my throat and slammed

me against the wall. His eyes were blood shot red and beads of sweat was gathered on his forehead. He was trying to instill fear in me, but the shit wasn't working. I could really give a fuck. This nigga was a clown as far as I was concerned.

"You can get all that leaving and being with the next man out of your head. We family now. It's 'til death do us part. I apologize for having to grab on you like this, but you talking crazy."

I did not flinch. I just stood motionless listening to this man plead his case.

"I'm sorry because I did fuck around with that girl. It was only a couple times, nothing serious. She was out of line saying a word to you, and she'll be dealt with accordingly. But baby, you can't let these scandalous hoes come in and ruin our happy home. They just jealous and sitting around waiting and plotting to take your place. I'm going to let go of your neck, but you have to promise me that you'll calm down and be mature about this shit."

I nodded my head yes. Nico released me from his grasp, and I sat down on the edge of the bed.

"So, what you want me to do Nico, act like you didn't cheat on me and have me out here looking foolish?"

Nico walked over to where I was sitting on the bed and knelt down on the floor next to me. He took my hand and continued to plead his case.

"Baby, I know that's easier said than done, but

I'm begging you to be the bigger person and let it go. I promise I won't fuck with her ever again. I made a mistake. I'm a man. I can admit that. I'm asking for your forgiveness. I promise I'll make it up to you."

Nico was making all sort of promises and his words sounded sincere, but the damage was done. He would've been better off denying the shit to the bitter end. Now I knew for a fact he lied and cheated on me, and he must be punished. If Nico thought he was just gonna slide through this like the snake that he was, he was in for a rude awaking. I would play the role of a dumb, dutiful girlfriend, but a bitch was about to make a move, one that Nico would never forget.

Deadly Design

For the next month Nico went into overdrive trying to persuade me to forgive him over the Porsha fiasco. It started with the keys to a brand-new AMG Benz delivered with a huge bow on top. Then he flew me to LA for a shopping spree on Rodeo Drive in Beverly Hills. Finally, we went on a romantic vacation to Antigua. After relaxing for a week, the night before we were leaving, during a candlelight dinner on the terrace, Nico got down on bended knee and slipped a massive diamond stunner on my finger. When he proposed, of course I accepted. He believed all was forgiven but as far as I was concerned, nothing had changed. I was secretly plotting the demise of Nico Carter.

The day after we got back from Antigua, I got dressed and headed out that evening to a lounge called Sunken Harbor Club. I got there early and had a seat at the end of the bar so I could get a clear view of my target. From what Inga told me, I knew that every Wednesday night around ten o'clock, Ritchie came here for a couple of drinks before handling his nighttime business. She also told me that as far as she knew, Nico never came with him.

About twenty minutes after I arrived, Ritchie came sauntering in solo. I knew he hadn't noticed me, so I walked around the back in the direction of the lady's restroom. When I saw where he positioned himself at the bar, I walked in a path that he would have to see me. As I made my way closer to him, I pretended to be looking in my purse for something. When I got right in front of his chair, Ritchie grabbed my arm.

"Precious, what you doin' in here?"

I glanced up and pretended to be startled and surprised to see Ritchie. "Oh, hey Ritchie. I was sup-posed to meet my cousin for a drink, but he just sent me a text and said he can't make it."

"Since you already here, why don't you have a drink with me. Unless you in a hurry."

I took a glimpse at my watch as if I might have someplace to be. "I guess I have time for one drink."

Several drinks later, Ritchie had his hand on my thigh. He was nice and tipsy, while I was very clear

headed. This slimy nigga was so busy trying to talk me out my panties that he didn't even realize I had been sipping on the same drink he ordered for me when I first sat down.

"Precious, you know the only reason I fucked wit' Inga was to get under your skin," he drunkenly confessed.

"Seriously? Why was you trying to get under my skin?" between him and Nico, I was mastering the art of playing dumb.

"You always acted so fuckin' uppity like a nigga was trash. I knew being wit' yo' best friend would piss you off. Inga is cool, but I settled since I couldn't have what I really wanted, which is you. If you were mine, I would neva play you out wit' a tired hoe like Porsha. I told Nico what a dumbass he was for doing that shit to you."

Ritchie tilted his head back as he took a shot of tequila. He put his glass down and stroked the side of my face. He thought that bullshit he spit impressed me. But Ritchie was a man, just like Nico, and he would stick his dick in the next bitch too. I always knew he was jealous of him. Before I cared out of concern for my man, but now I cared because I would use it to my advantage to make Nico pay.

"I appreciate you looking out for me, Ritchie. I'll admit I was a little hard on you, but I think it was be-cause I was attracted to you too. I did feel some kinda way when you started dating Inga."

"I knew it! I knew it!" he belted as he slammed his fist on the bar. "Baby, I knew you wanted me just as much as I wanted you."

Ritchie was a bigger clown than I thought. Even though in my mind the relationship between Nico and I was over, he was still a way better man than Ritchie could ever be.

"Ritchie, why don't we leave here so we can have some privacy. I would hate for one of Nico's people to spot us."

"Fuck Nico. He don't run me."

"Baby, I know, but he is still my man. I don't want no drama."

"If I have my way, he won't be your man for long," Ritchie asserted before he paid the bill and we left.

When we arrived at Ritchie's place, I guided him straight to the bedroom so we could get right to it. I didn't want to waste any time as this was a work assignment not a love connection. I led him to the large bed in the center of the bedroom. I planned on riding his dick real hard for a good ten minutes so he would cum fast, and then break the fuck out. But Ritchie wanted to try and seduce a bitch. He lit candles and had soft, seductive music playing. He laid me on his bed and ate my pussy for about fifteen minutes, trying to make me have an orgasm. I guess he thought it would get me open on him. But unfortunately, he

couldn't even eat coochie better than Nico. Trying to speed the process up, I faked an orgasm, so he would get his face out my pussy. I had to be home in an hour, because I didn't want Nico to start getting suspicious and asking me a million questions.

Finally, we got down to it. The outside light was shining through a huge window, showing the silhouette of my naked body as I straddled Ritchie. I had that nigga screaming my name. Inga was right, he was working with a nice-sized tool, but he still disgusted me, so I couldn't enjoy it. It didn't matter because this was work, so I treated it accordingly. He lasted five minutes longer than I expected, but once he came, he was out like a light. After fixing myself up, I jumped in my car and drove home.

When I arrived home last night Nico was still out, so I took a shower and went to bed. In the morning, I was awakened because I heard him on the phone yelling at somebody. I only caught the tail end.

"Yo stop fuckin' up and get the shit done!" Nico's voice thundered through the bedroom as he threw the phone on the bed. He was standing in the doorway, visibly upset, cursing under his breath. I got out the bed and walked over to him.

"Baby, what's wrong?"

"Ritchie stupid ass. He was supposed to handle some important shit for me last night, but he said he fell asleep. That nigga my righthand man. How the fuck is he gonna drop the ball when it comes to makin' money?"

Nico shook his head in frustration and sat down on the chair. I stood behind him and massaged his shoulders.

"Don't let Ritchie stress you out. It'll be alright. Relax."

Nico closed his eyes while I continued to give him a massage. "That feels good. Yeah, right there. You always know how to give me exactly what I need."

"That's what I'm here for. I wanna take your mind off everything." I stopped massaging Nico's shoulders and massaged his manhood with my mouth. He was moaning and pulling my hair tightly because it was feeling so good to him. My mind began wondering if he moaned the same way when Porsha was deep throating his dick.

I couldn't front this shit had me full of rage and disdain. I saw the bitch, and no, she didn't look better than me, and no, she didn't have a better body than me. But I had to question if she could fuck better than me. Only Nico knew the answer to that, and of course, he wasn't going to give it.

This was all the more reason why I had to bring him to his knees, because this nigga had me questioning myself as a woman. And if the next bitch pussy

was better than mine. That was too many things. But I would never share all these insecurities with Nico. This was pain I would bear alone. My plan was to convince him that all was forgiven and forgotten. He would believe that this drama only made our bond tighter, and no matter what, I would ride for him. That way, Nico will never be prepared when it all falls down.

Idols Become Rivals

Ritchie and I began having secret sexual tryst three times a week. If he had his way, it would've been every day. He kept demanding that I stop dealing with Nico and be his girl. His ego and being open on some new pussy had made him delusional.

I was not going to allow a lame nigga to fuck up my plans, so I constantly stroked Ritchie's ego and assured him we would be together, I just needed more time. He didn't even care that his friendship with Nico would be over, because he was never Nico's friend to begin with. I had to remind him that I did care about my friendship with Inga, and she would be devastated. I was on my way to pick her up and it would be my first time seeing her since I started creeping with Ritchie. While driving I was getting lost in my thoughts when CoCo Jones ICU came on.

Something 'bout your hands on my body
Feels better than any man I ever met
Something 'bout the way you just get me
I try and I don't 'cause I can't forget
You've got a feeling, a soul that I need in my life...

I was unable to listen to the song and turned the volume all the way down. Not long ago I felt that way about Nico, but he destroyed whatever we could've been. I no longer gave a fuck about him, but Inga was just an innocent casualty in all this. When shit did blow up, I hoped she would understand and not take it personal.

When I pulled up in front of the projects where Inga lived, she was standing outside and obviously upset.

"What has you riled up?" I wanted to know as we both leaned against my car.

"You mean who. Ritchie dumb ass. He been so anal lately. Every time I ask him for something, he bite my head off. He don't hardly even fuck me no more. I believe that nigga might be open on some other bitch, 'cause his attitude is stank as shit. But whoever she is gonna be mad about it 'cause I'm pregnant." Inga's tone was boastful and defiant.

"Pregnant, you sure?"

"Girl, yes. Nine weeks. I took the home test and went to the clinic yesterday to be sure."

"Did you tell Ritchie yet?"

"Nope."

"Inga, do you really wanna have his baby? You just said ya having problems, and you think he's open on some other chick."

"I know, but the baby might make him act right. When I become Ritchie's baby mama, he ain't gon' have no choice but to take care of me and his child. I'm tired of living in these projects."

"I don't know if tryna lock Ritchie down wit' a baby is the right move. A nigga ain't gotta walk around wit' his belly poked out for all those months. Ritchie will still be runnin' the streets, so while you think you trapping him, you only trapping yourself. And if you believe that paper gonna be right, remember, Ritchie is a street nigga. His money is illegal. It ain't like you can take his ass to court and ball out on a whole bunch of child support. This won't be no million-dollar baby."

"I hear you, but I ain't got a whole lot of options. I have a better chance of Ritchie staying with me if I have his baby. A nigga be having a soft spot for they first born, especially if it's a boy. Once the baby is here, he'll always have a reason to come back to me."

"That's the same thing that every other baby mama living in the hood thought. But once little Ray Ray get about three and his daddy ain't nowhere to be seen, the only thing they be waiting on is that EBT card. I would hate for you to be one of them, Inga."

"It'll be different for me. You'll see." Inga tried to

convince me with little to no confidence in her voice.

The news that my best friend just dropped on me could've easily put a monkey wrench in my plans, but I refused to let it. I told Inga from day one not to get caught up in Ritchie, let alone have a baby with him. Her stupidity wasn't going to interfere with my scheme.

After I left from speaking with Inga, I stopped by my moms' crib to give her some money and make sure won't no bum nigga residing with her. When I was leaving about to get in my car, another car pulled up beside me, and Ritchie was on the passenger side.

"What's up baby, what you doing over here?"

"I was just buying some smoke."

I couldn't take the chance of Ritchie knowing where my mom's lived in case things didn't work out the way I planned. His snake ass would come over tryna shake my mother down.

"Oh, I coulda hooked you up. Am I gonna see you later on tonight?" he asked sounding his normal thirsty self.

"I'm not sure. Nico been trippin' about why I be gone so much lately."

While I was speaking with Ritchie, I noticed the driver had put his phone down. He seemed familiar to me, but I couldn't figure out why until he turned around to retrieve something from the backseat. I immediately recognized the unforgettable scar on his left cheek. Chills went down my spine, but I kept a poker face not to show I recognized Azar's killer.

"Baby, I need to be wit' you. Make it happen. Please." Ritchie's begging snapped me out my thoughts.

"I'll try."

"Yo, you seen that little bag of weed I had in the car?" Azar's killer asked. Hearing his voice instantly brought back dreadful memories from that night and my close encounter with death.

"I put it in the glove compartment. But Butch man, you don't need to be smokin' 'round here. We got guns and shit in the car. Them boys in blue is out heavy tonight. Weed might be legal but they'll still use that shit as an excuse to pull us over," Ritchie warned him.

"Ritchie, I gotta go. I'll call you later. I promise."

"You better!" he called out.

I quickly got in my car. Before I drove off, I stared in the rearview mirror to get one last look at Azar's killer, who I now knew was a nigga named Butch. He probably didn't know who I was, because when he put the gun to the back of my head, my hair was in a slick bun. Right now, my hair was hanging loose and curly.

Finding out that Ritchie was hanging with a shady nigga like Butch had my mind spinning. The reason all that shit went down with Azar was because Butch and his people fronted on his money and stole his drugs. If Ritchie was doing business with him, I

doubted Nico knew anything about it as he was selective with who he broke bread with. I needed to further investigate, as I did not want any hiccups with my plan to teach Nico the ultimate lesson.

I needed to know if whatever Ritchie was scheming on with Butch would be problematic for Nico, so for the last few days anything business related had my full attention. One afternoon when I came home, Nico was in his office with the door partially open. I was posted up in the hallway trying to ear hustle but got distracted when I felt my phone vibrating. It was Inga with a 911 text. I rushed to the bedroom to call her back.

Inga was hollering and carrying on when she answered the phone, barely audible. "What's wrong are you okay?" I asked closing the bedroom door. Instantly I thought that Ritchie sold me out and confessed everything to her.

"No! I just got home. Would you please come over? I finally told Ritchie about the baby, and he flipped the fuck out."

"Say no more. I'm on the way." I was relieved Ritchie hadn't blown up my spot, but I was also concerned about Inga.

She was distraught when I got to her apartment.

Inga was pacing back and forth in the living room, going from cursing loudly to then crying hysterically before finally spilling what went down.

"I can't believe Ritchie's foul ass. When I told him I was pregnant he smacked the shit outta me."

Inga turned her head to show me the bruise on her face. The damage Ritchie inflicted on Inga had me livid.

"That muthafucker!" I seethed.

"He said he ain't gon' be trapped by a baby wit' a bitch he don't even want. Then he told me that if I didn't have an abortion, he would cut the baby out of me himself. Can you believe that monster!"

"Inga, I'm so sorry." I held her close for a moment. "What you gon' do?" we sat down on the couch. I had never seen Inga this upset. All I wanted to do was calm her down.

"I don't know. I really want to have my baby. Not just because of Ritchie, but I ain't got nothing else going on wit' my life. Having a baby will change all that."

"You know I got your back no matter what decision you make, but are you ready to be a mother? Especially now that Ritchie has made his position clear."

"Fuck Ritchie! I don't want nothing but his money to take care of our baby. You were right about him. He's a snake." From there, Inga had diarrhea of the mouth. "I don't know if you've noticed, but lately Ritchie and Nico ain't been hanging. Ritchie been tight wit' some

new kid named Butch."

My ears perked up. I had to dive in and see if Inga could divulge any new information to me. "Who's Butch?"

"Exactly," Inga said, signaling to me we were on the same page. "When I asked Ritchie, he told me to mind my business. That made me even more curious. The other night when Ritchie thought I was sleep, I heard a knock at the door. At first, I thought it was a bitch because Ritchie don't like nobody to know where he lives. I went to the top of the stairs being nosey, and I caught sight of a nigga with the most horrific scar on the side of his face. When I heard Ritchie call him Butch, I realized that was the nigga he been on the phone wit' all the time. Precious, I swear they was talking about fuckin' Nico over on some serious paper. Like a mil. Ritchie tried to say that's a sprinkle for Nico, but it would start an all-out war."

"So, Ritchie trying to take Nico out without getting any blood on his own hands?"

"Facts. I did some asking around and that nigga Butch used to be a low-level stickup kid, then graduated to robbing niggas for large amount of drugs. Somehow, he managed not to get smoked and has made some major moves. But he's a snake just like Ritchie. You betta warn Nico that Ritchie ain't his friend, he's the opp."

"I will," I said, knowing I had no intentions of alerting Nico to what Ritchie was plotting. "With the info you just dropped on me, I need to get home and talk to Nico."

"Of course. Go handle that."

"You should go stay at a hotel for a couple days and buy some things you need," I said reaching in my purse, taking out several hundreds of dollars. I handed the money to Inga. Her eyes lit up.

"Thanks for looking out Precious." This was the first time Inga smiled since I got here.

"Always. Please make sure you keep a low profile for the next few days. Once I warn Nico, he'll handle Ritchie accordingly. I don't want you anywhere around when this shit blows up."

It all made sense now, I thought to myself after I left Inga's apartment. I began wondering exactly when Ritchie started planning the murder of his best friend. Was it before or after he fell in love with the pussy? Right now, it was irrelevant. I needed to figure out my next move. I'd been waiting to blow up Nico's world once I had stacked a hundred thousand dollars, but now I had an opportunity to walk away with a cool million. With that type of money, I could leave Brooklyn and start my life over. But I needed to act fast. Me and Ritchie were both determined to take Nico down, but I planned to be the only one left standing once the smoke cleared.

Collision Course

It took a few days but my ear hustling finally paid off. I got home earlier than expected and Nico was in his office with the door wide open. I couldn't hear what the person on the other end was saying, but there was no need because Nico gave me all the intel I needed.

"There's potential to make a shitload of money with this new connect Ritchie linked me up with. This first round I committed to a million to see if the streets say it's as good as he claims. But I have a few things I need to handle tonight, so I need you to stop by the warehouse, get the money and bring it here. That way in the morning when I link up with Ritchie, we can go straight to the connect and make the exchange."

I was salivating at the mouth at the thought of getting my hands on that money. A million-dollar coup wasn't part of my initial plan, but it was now. As Nico finished up his call, I tiptoed upstairs to the bedroom making sure not to be seen or heard.

When he finally came upstairs, I was just getting out the shower and he was obviously surprised to see me.

"Baby, I didn't even know you were home," he said as I saw his dick rise up from looking at my naked wet body.

"When I got here, I didn't see you, so I just came straight to the bedroom to take a shower. I was tired and ready for bed."

"I hope not too tired to let me feel inside of you." Nico's eyes were consumed with lust, and I decided to allow him to taste it one last time since he'd never feel the inside of my pussy again. He lifted my body up, carrying me over to the bed, and we made love. After we finished, I laid in his arms. I had to admit that nobody could fuck me like Nico, but oh well, sex isn't everything.

Right when I stood up to go to the bathroom, I heard the doorbell ring. "Baby, you want me to get the door."

"Nah, that's just Tommy dropping off some pa-perwork. I'll be back."

Yeah, some paperwork in the form of a million dollars, I thought to myself. Nico quickly put on his clothes to go answer the door. Within a few minutes he was back but empty handed.

"That was fast," I remarked getting back in the bed.

"I told you Tommy was just dropping off some paperwork before I left out to handle some business."

"Oh, I didn't realize you're going back out. How are things between you and Ritchie?" I questioned with indifference. "I haven't heard you mention him lately. Is there still tension?"

"Nah, we worked it out. You know we brothers; it's 'til death do us part. Just like with us. I'll be home late so don't wait up."

Nico came over to the bed and kissed me on the lips. His mouth was soft and warm. As he was about to walk away, I pulled him back, to give him one final kiss goodbye. That chapter of him being my man was now closed. Once alone, I immediately started getting my shit together because I was working on borrowed time. I wasn't sure if I was going to be able to come back for the rest of my belongings so I gathered up as much of my stuff as I could in order of importance, starting with all my jewelry (including Nico's), furs, designer bags, shoes and then clothes. Once I got all that in the car, I went downstairs to the basement.

Nico had no idea I discovered his hidden compartment in the basement. I actually found it by accident when he was out of town and there was a power outage. While I was in the basement looking for the breaker panel, I tripped. I aimed the flashlight on the floor to see what I bumped into, and it was a large metal storage bin. When I opened the clasp there was money and a gun inside. There wasn't much paper, so

I left it there. Plus, I didn't want Nico to know I located his stash in case I needed it for whatever reason in the future. Well, that reason had presented itself.

When I opened the clasp on the metal bin there was a large duffel bag inside. Once I unzipped it, my eyes were twinkling and my smile beaming seeing all that cash. The gun was still there, which I grabbed just in case I needed protection. After doing one more house search to make sure I wasn't forgetting anything, I made my escape.

My next move was to call Ritchie. When he answered he sounded like he was in the middle of something.

"Yo."

"Ritchie, I need to see you."

"I'm busy right now. You gonna have to wait."

"I can't! It's important. It's about Nico."

"What about Nico... did you tell him about us?" he sounded tense.

"Listen, I need to see you. It can't wait." I said, ignoring his question.

"A'ight. Meet me at my crib in a half."

I knew Ritchie was shook and stressed, wondering if I ran my mouth to Nico, messing up the bloodshed he was plotting to start on his own. After I hung up with Ritchie, I immediately called Nico to execute my next strategic chess move.

"What's up, baby."

"I was calling to tell you goodbye."

"What you mean goodbye? Where you going?"

"I can't do this anymore."

"Do what?"

"I tried to put the whole Porsha situation behind me, but I couldn't. The only person that was able to comfort me through my pain was Ritchie."

"What the fuck did you just say?"

"Nico, I've been seeing Ritchie for a few months now, and we're in love. I'm pregnant with his baby." I sniffled, pretending to hold back tears, while I parked across the street from Ritchie's place. Luckily, it was dark outside, so he didn't notice me when he pulled up and went inside.

"Precious, don't fuckin' play wit' me. This shit ain't funny."

"It's not meant to be. You shoulda never let me find out you were fuckin' around wit' that basic bird Porsha. You hurt me and made me look like a weak bitch in the process. For that reason, I'm done wit' you and I'm moving on with your best friend."

"Where the fuck are you right now?"

"Ritchie's crib."

"I'ma give you one more chance to take all this bullshit back before I lose it."

"I can't take it back, because it's the truth. Why do you think Ritchie was actin' so foul towards you. He couldn't stand the fact that I refused to leave you. But once I found out I was pregnant, I decided it was time to let you go."

"That might be my seed. How you know I'm not the father?"

"I can promise you, you're not the father. The baby I'm carrying is Ritchie's."

"Then you a dead bitch." Nico warned, ending the call.

I pulled my car in front of Ritchie's house in plain view for Nico to see. I grabbed the gun and walked across the street, hiding beside a house under construction.

Within fifteen minutes, Nico came flying down the street in his SUV and parked beside my car. He jumped out in a rage, clutching his own gun as he sprinted towards Ritchie's place, running up the stairs. He banged on the door with gun drawn, and when Ritchie opened it, probably thinking it was me, all I heard was Nico screaming, "Where the fuck is Precious at?" before the door slammed shut.

Moments later, I saw another car coming down the street. As the car got closer, I realized it was Butch and I had to act fast. There was no way I could let him interfere with what was going on between Nico and Ritchie. I snuck around the back of the house under construction and ducked behind another car before sneaking across the street. Butch was on the phone, so he was distracted. Once he ended the call and was under the darkness of Ritchie's walkway, I made my move. As if he felt my presence, Butch turned around to be greeted with the barrel of my gun pointing

directly at him.

"This is for Azar."

I busted off two gunshots, never allowing him to utter one word. As the bullets exploded through his chest, Butch fell backwards, landing on the bottom step being killed instantly. I walked up to him and put one more bullet in Butch's face, guaranteeing he wouldn't have an open casket. Seconds later, I heard gunshots coming from inside Ritchie's place, signaling me to make my next call.

"Yes, I heard several gunshots coming from 218 Adelphi Street. I think somebody has been murdered." I ended the call and placed the phone next to Butch's dead body.

My heart was racing. It wasn't because I had just murdered somebody; it was the adrenaline of seeing my plan materialize. I prayed that the gunshots I heard coming from Ritchie's house were that of Nico murdering him. If they weren't, everything would be ruined. I wanted Ritchie dead and Nico locked up suffering for betraying me.

Laying Low

Before I was two blocks away from Ritchie's house, I saw police cars speeding down the street. I knew within minutes the street would be blocked off, and at least one murder investigation would be underway, hopefully two. Although I liked having the gun I took from Nico for protection, I had to get rid of it now since Butch's body was on it and probably a few more.

I drove across the bridge to the city and tossed the gun in the Hudson River. I then drove back to Brooklyn and went to the hotel where Inga was staying. I took a deep breath then knocked on the door. Inga opened the door munching on some snacks oblivious that both our lives were forever changed tonight.

"Girl, I was surprised when you called saying you were on your way over. Nico gon' start trippin' if you don't get home soon."

"I know, so I'm not gonna stay that long. I just wanted to bring you something."

"What?" she asked as I followed Inga over to the sitting area.

"Take this." I unzipped my LV backpack and pulled out a large envelope handing it to Inga. "It's fifty thousand. It's to help you maintain yourself for a minute. I also put the keys to my apartment on Riverside Drive in the envelope. The rent is paid up for the year. This will help give you a start. You and the baby."

"Damn Precious, you a real one." Inga's eyes teared up and she hugged me tighter than I've ever been held in my life.

"I better be going. You know how Nico can get."

"Precious, thank you for everything. We appreciate you." Inga put her hand on her stomach. She looked down and smiled, rubbing her slightly protruding belly.

I walked out of that hotel room, not knowing when I would see Inga again. I didn't give her that money because I felt guilty about fucking with Ritchie. I just wanted her seed to be OK. I knew Inga would have that baby because she didn't understand the survival of the streets. Just because you come from the hood and see how hard it is to have something; it doesn't mean you comprehend the struggle. Inga never understood, but I hoped with the money I gave her and the crib, she would try to give her baby a better life than the one we had growing up.

It was essential to make my escape out of Brooklyn fast, so I took it over to Jersey. I'd only been there a couple of times, but I did remember it was nothing like New York. I checked in at the W Hoboken. When I got in my room, it was one of those elevated suites with stunning panoramic views of the Manhattan skyline and Hudson River. I stood on the sprawling private terrace, and I thought about Butch's murder weapon being somewhere in that big body of water.

I then got undressed, and since it was too late to watch the news, I took a hot shower and fell into a deep sleep. I didn't wake up until late in the afternoon, and the first thing I checked was my cell phone. I had no missed calls or messages. There was no local news on the television, nothing but soaps, and talk shows. Waiting to see what happened was driving me crazy. I ordered room service thinking that eating some food would minimize my anxiety. Two more hours passed, and I decided I needed some fresh air. I also needed to find a storage facility and meet up with a guy I knew to get another gun. With all the drama I had going on, it was imperative to keep protection on me at all times.

Immediately after securing a storage facility to store the majority of my belongings, I headed over to Harlem to meet up with this dude who could put

any weapon you desired directly in your hand. I made my purchase, broke out and headed back to my hotel room. I turned on the television to catch the six o'clock news not feeling optimistic I would find out anything, but then my patients paid off when a reporter was on the scene discussing the shooting:

This is Steve Douglass reporting live from Fort Greene. The house behind me is the crime scene of a double homicide that occurred late last night. The two male victims have yet to be identified, but cops do have a suspect in custody. His name is Nico Carter, a purported notorious drug kingpin...

Not caring to hear anything else I switched off the television and flopped down on the bed. "YES!" I echoed as I spread my entire body across the bed. I finally felt some sort of justice. Even so, I wouldn't be completely satisfied until Nico was doing life behind bars. In one night, I was able to get rid of the three people I hated most in this world. But the punishment Nico would soon endure was the sweetest.

If the system prevailed, he would spend the rest of his life locked up, knowing his fiancée was fucking his best friend behind his back, and believing that I was actually pregnant by Ritchie. That was enough to make any man want to get a hold of a bed sheet and hang himself inside his jail cell. Nico had too much pride to ever commit suicide, so he would have no choice but to spend his days and nights in confinement visualizing Ritchie twisting my back out and wondering if I screamed his name and called him daddy the way I did with him. Good for that muthafucker.

While celebrating, I kept checking my phone. I was surprised that still nobody called me about Nico. I knew the streets had to be on fire that the chosen one was now in police custody for murder. The only person I really expected to call me was Inga. Bree would never discuss that shit with me over the phone. I decided to lay low but keep my ears to the streets.

Unwavering Love

When I tell you the streets were silent. I had to do my own detective work to find out Nico had an upcoming arraignment. I was sure he would be seeking bail but for felony murder charges I highly doubted it would be granted. The local state and Federal government have had a hard-on for Nico for so many years. Never did they think they would nab him for murdering his best friend. If they had their way, Nico Carter wouldn't ever see the light of day, at least that was what I was counting on.

However, I couldn't take any chances. I continued to lay low until the court date finally arrived. Since I would be in Brooklyn, and I hadn't seen my mom in a minute, I decided to stop by her apartment to see how she was doing before I headed to court. Last time I saw her, she was in a bad way and her steady decline was becoming more rapid.

Before I could finish my thoughts, my iPhone started ringing and it was Inga. "What's up, Inga?" I said calmly. I wasn't in the mood to speak to her, but I needed to hear as much street gossip as possible.

"Precious, did you hear about Ritchie?" Inga bawled. By the tears that were obviously flowing, she sounded as if she only recently heard about the murders.

"Yeah, you just hearing about it?"

"Hmm hum. That night when I saw you, the next morning I had to go to the hospital. I was having real bad cramps in my stomach and there was a little bit of blood. They finally released me today."

"Did you lose the baby?"

"No, the baby is fine. The doctor told me I'ma have to take it easy throughout my pregnancy. I'm glad I have a part of Ritchie growing inside of me now that he gone."

"With Ritchie being dead you still want to have his baby?" I asked while saying to myself, this *is a dumb bitch.*

"Yeah. I know Ritchie was foul, but I loved him. I guess you told Nico that Ritchie was tryna to set him up. That's why he killed him."

"Inga, I neva even had a chance. When I got home that night, Nico was already gone. I didn't even know what happened until I heard it on the news."

"Well, he must've found out some other way. Ritchie's stupid ass should've neva crossed Nico. But

I can't believe Nico's in jail. You must be devastated, Precious. I know how much you love him."

"So much is going on, I really haven't had time to take it all in."

"Have you spoken to Nico?"

"No, I haven't been staying at home. I wasn't sure if the cops was gonna run up in there or something."

"That's true. I heard Nico supposed to have a bail hearing today."

"Where you hear that from?" I pretended not to be privy to that information, although I planned on being there.

"This girl named Vanika."

"Who that?"

"She Corey's sister. Corey a little nigga. He works for one of Nico's street lieutenants."

"What else she say?"

"Not too much. Just that everybody stressed 'cause wit' Nico locked up and Ritchie dead; they don't have nobody to lead the way. Them two was the only ones that dealt one on one wit' the connect. Ain't nobody heard from Nico. They don't know if the police ain't letting him make no phone calls or what. That's why I was wondering if you spoke to him."

"Not yet."

"So, are you gonna go to court for his bail hearing today?"

"I don't know. Nico might want me to keep a low profile."

"That's true. Wit' Nico locked up, I'll understand if you'll need your apartment back."

"Nah, don't worry about it. I'll make some other arrangements."

"I know you ain't going back to your moms' crib?"

"Nope." Inga had me feeling she was the police with all these simple-ass questions she was spitting at me.

"So, what do..."

"Yo, I gotta go. I'll be in touch," I said, abruptly ending the call. There was nothing left to discuss with Inga because she gave me all the pertinent information she had. The rest of the conversation would've consisted of her picking my brain, which was out of the question. I continued on my way to see my mom, pushing Inga out of my mind.

When I entered my mom's apartment, I immediately stepped back out, closed the door and double checked the apartment number to make sure I was at the right crib. I reopened the door and was in disbelief at how clean the place was. The walls were freshly painted, the hardwood floors had been refinished and the whole apartment had new furniture. It didn't even look like the same place. I opened the refrigerator and not a bottle of liquor was in sight. Nothing but juice, water,

fruit and other healthy foods, which made me wonder if my mom had died and someone else took over her apartment. The typically nasty, unkept apartment was pristine.

"Precious, I wasn't expecting to see you today, but I'm glad you're here."

When I turned around to face her, my heart almost stopped. I stood for a few moments speechless. I couldn't get over how beautiful my mother looked. She picked up weight and her hourglass shape was still intact. Her skin was glowing, and her sandy brown hair was cut short and streaked with blonde highlights. It made her green eyes stand out even more. All the beauty that was hidden because of drugs and alcohol was now shining through. It was amazing. I just hugged her and wouldn't let go. For the first time in my life, I had a mother.

"That's some hug. Are you okay?" my mother asked stroking my hair.

"What happened to you?"

"I took your advice and got myself together. I started an outpatient treatment program. I've been clean for two months now."

"I'm so proud of you. For the first time in my life, I have a mother. I wish I could hold you like this forever." I smiled and held my mother close in my arms once again.

"I pray one day you can forgive me for everything I put you through."

"Say less. You're already forgiven as I never stopped loving you. I hate to leave you because we have so much to celebrate. But there's an arraignment hearing for one of Inga's close friends, and I promised her I would attend since she can't be there."

"How is Inga doing?"

"Inga's good. She's actually pregnant. Very soon she'll be a mommy."

"Tell her I said congratulations and make sure she brings the baby over to see me."

"Will do. And mom, I really am proud of you, and you look so beautiful. I'll be back tomorrow. I love you." We held hands as my mom walked me to the door.

"I love you more," my mother said kissing me on my cheek before we said goodbye.

That short period of time I just spent with my mother was the happiest moment of my life. I decided that when I found a house in Jersey, I was bringing my mother with me. We could both leave Brooklyn and start over together. Maybe even open up a beauty salon, nail spa, or clothing boutique together. We would be the hottest mother and daughter duo ever. My existence in this world finally had meaning.

Ex For A Reason

Wrapped up planning a new future with my mother, I lost track of time. I looked at my watch and realized I had to hurry and get to court. I parked, rushed upstairs to enter the courtroom where I was told the hearing would be taking place. When I creeped inside, I sat in the back not wanting to be seen. Nico's arraignment hearing was already underway. He was standing next to his high-profile attorney, looking prouder than ever, even in his jail jumpsuit.

The prosecutor argued that bail shouldn't be set for Nico, not only because of the heinous nature of the crime, but because it was also a double homicide. He further stated that Nico was a flight risk, and due to his illegal drug activity, was a menace to society.

Nico's attorney argued that Nico was an upstanding businessman in the community and that he acted in self-defense. They went back and forth, and in the end the judge sided with the prosecution and denied bail. Nico's attorney immediately demanded that his client wanted a speedy trial.

Once the judge gave his ruling, I quietly got up to leave when I heard someone say, "Precious, is that you?" I tried to step up my speed, but then they got louder. "Precious Cummings, is that you?" I turned to see who had blown my cover, and instantly Nico and I made eye contact. If looks could kill, I would've died that morning at 120 Schermerhorn Street in the Brooklyn Courthouse. Nico stared at me until the bailiff took him away.

I rushed out in a panic. Trailing behind me, I heard the person who blew up my spot still calling my name. I looked back and realized it was some random girl I went to high school with. Two steps behind her, was Porsha. Even to court, that bird ass bitch, didn't know how to represent. She had on some low-cut pink dress that was made so cheaply, if you pulled one piece of thread, the whole ensemble would fall apart. Yet, she was strutting through the courthouse believing she looked like a snack.

Seeing Porsha confirmed that Nico was getting exactly what he deserved. He was still seeing that bitch after he swore, he was done with her. Niggas weren't shit. While I was already vexed, Porsha approached me dripping with anger.

"What are you doing here? You know Nico don't wanna see you!"

"Get out my face before I lay hands on you."

"You have no reason to be here," Porsha snapped.

"Listen, I'm not gonna discuss my relationship wit' my fiancée with you." I flaunted the massive engagement ring Nico have given me all up in Porsha's face. "So, as you can see, I have every reason to be here."

"Ain't nobody stuttin' you, Precious."

"Clearly you are, as you sound salty. Whateva you got going on wit' Nico is cool 'cause you ain't nothing but a broke down, raggedy, bootleg version of what I'll neva be. So, step the fuck off before I put my foot back on yo' throat and stomp that ass one more time."

"You a dead bitch. A dead bitch!" Porsha repeated.

I balled up my fist ready to fight Porsha in the middle of the courthouse.

"Miss, calm down!" a security officer intervened and caught my swing mid-air. He held my arms gently, wanting to deescalate the situation.

"Nah, let her go. I wish you would put yo' hands on me, Precious!" Porsha raged, trying to taunt me.

"I'm going to ask you to leave this area now, before I cite you for disorderly conduct," he warned as Porsha rolled her eyes, pointing her finger in my direction.

"Officer, you can let me go. I'm not gonna lay hands on this raggedy hoe. You wanna act like you Nico's wife. Then you can do that bid wit' him like you his wife too."

"Fuck you, Precious," Porsha shot back and stormed off.

"Listen, take my advice; calm down and leave without having another altercation with that woman. She's not worth it. Next time I might not be here to stop you, and it could be you in front of that judge."

I was breathing so hard. I felt like that bitch was threatening my life. Consumed with anger, I simply nodded my head, knowing what the security guard said was true. I got my bearings together and left.

While I was driving back to the hotel, Inga's name popped up on my car's infotainment screen. I figured Porsha must've told Tanisha's cousin about our encounter at the courthouse earlier today and Inga was calling to get the dirt from me. "Hello."

"What up, Precious?"

"The same bullshit from when I spoke to you this morning. Nothing's changed. Just handling some things. I'm kinda busy. What's up?"

"Oh, where you at?"

"In the streets."

"You in Brooklyn?"

"Nah, that's not what I said. I'm in the streets," I replied, feeling funny about how Inga was coming at me.

"So, when you coming back to Brooklyn, 'cause I wanted to see you?"

"I'm not sure. You haven't been staying at my place in Harlem."

"No. Wit' the pregnancy and all, my mom wanted me to be close by family."

"That's cool."

"Do you want to stop by and pick up your apartment keys since I won't be staying there?"

"I'm good. I have an extra set. Inga, I hate to cut this short, but like I said, I'm in the middle of handling some things. We'll get up later." That nauseating feeling was coming over me, but I tried to shake it off as just being overwhelmed by seeing Nico and my confrontation with Porsha.

When I got to my hotel room, I took a shower wanting to wash away my stressful day. Now that I got confirmation Nico wasn't getting out on bail it was time I put Brooklyn and everything it represented behind me. From this moment on, I was putting this shit with Nico in my rearview mirror and looking forward to sharing this new journey with my mother.

Shattered World

I drove up to the housing projects looking forward to seeing my mother. I sat in my car for a few minutes, getting my thoughts together. I was excited about sharing the news I wanted her to move to Jersey with me. But then I also debated if I needed to reveal all the chaos I set in motion and how I planned to walk away from it unscathed. I decided to wait and discuss the last part another day. My mother finally got her life together and this evening was a time for us to celebrate new beginnings, not burden her with my drama.

I had a beautiful bouquet of flowers in one hand and non-alcoholic champagne in the other to honor my mother's sobriety. When I opened the apartment door, it was pitch black, which was unusual. My mother never went to bed before midnight, and she always fell asleep on the living room couch with the television on.

I turned on the light switch and to my despair the entire place had been ransacked. The brand-new couch my mother purchased was cut up. The kitchen cabinets were open with broken dishes everywhere. The plants that were in the window had been knocked down, and dirt was covering the floor. I walked slowly towards the hallway and saw the words *You're A Dead Bitch,* written on the walls.

My entire body went weak. I dropped the flowers and the champagne bottle crashed to the floor. I had to place my hand against the wall to hold myself up. I became flooded with the most agonizing sharp pain I've ever experienced. At that moment, I knew my life had forever changed.

I hesitated even entering my mother's room because reality would truly set in. Her door was slightly ajar. When I pushed it completely open, I saw my beautiful mother's body lying there on the bed with her head completely severed. My knees buckled and I fell to the floor. For the first time, since I was a little girl, I cried. The tears flowed, and they wouldn't stop.

It was as if all the heartache and pain from so many years scoured out begging to be released. I not only cried for myself, but I cried for my mother, the mother that I just found only yesterday. Now she'd been taken away from me before I could enjoy the mother and daughter moments that I dreamed of having all my life. Dreams that I never believed could be possible and now they wouldn't be. The shimmer of hope my mother gave me when I looked into her vibrant eyes yesterday had died with her.

On my way back to Jersey, I contemplated ending my life, by driving off the side of the road. The only thing that stopped me was that I didn't have the guts. With all the bullshit I'd seen and done, I was scared to end it all. My emotions had me in a chokehold. Revenge on Nico caused the death of my mother, and I was riddled with guilt. I would never be able to live that down.

When I made it back to the hotel room, I raided the mini bar and guzzled down every ounce of alcohol available. I needed to numb the pain. Between drinks, I cried, begged for forgiveness, questioned why my mother had to die and I was still alive, until I passed out surrounded by empty bottles of liquor.

"Fuck," I kept mumbling when the ringing of my phone wouldn't stop. "Yeah."

"Precious wake up!" I heard Inga yelling through the phone.

"I'm up. What is it?"

"Precious, I have something to tell you." There was silence on the phone for a few seconds. "Precious are you there?"

"Yeah, what do you have to tell me?"

"It's about your mother."

"What about my mother?" I asked, not wanting Inga to have a clue I already knew.

"She's dead, Precious. She was murdered some-

time last night."

"Not my mother. Do they have any idea who did it or why?"

"No, but because of the profession she was in, they thinking it could've been anybody."

"My mother had cleaned her life up. She wasn't in that profession no more, so tell them cops and anybody else that's runnin' they mouth, to shut the fuck up. They don't know nothin' about my mother. She better than all of them!" I screamed, defending my mother in death, since she was never defended in life.

"Precious, I'm sorry. I had no idea yo' moms turned her life around."

"How would you know?" I responded sarcastically.

"So, when you coming back to Brooklyn?"

"Inga, I don't fuckin' know. Maybe neva. Coming through BK seems like a death sentence to me. I don't want no parts of Brooklyn right now."

"So, where you gon' go?"

"Why the fuck you keep asking me so many damn questions? You been coming at me like you the feds since you called about Nico's arrest."

"Damn Precious, you my best friend. Excuse me for worrying about you."

"You got enough to worry about. Focus on that baby growing inside you, instead of wondering when the next time I'm stopping through Brooklyn."

"You know what, Precious, I know emotionally

you fucked up in the game right now. First, Nico get locked up and now your mom get murdered. That's a lot to deal wit', so I'm not gonna take none of the shit you saying personally. Just know I'm here if you need anything."

"Yeah, I hear you, Inga, but unless you can bring my mother back to life, what I need, you can't give me. I'll speak to you later."

A week later I found myself standing in the shadows at the graveside burial service for my mother. There was a small group of people including Bree, who remembered how beautiful and special my mother was at one time in her life, showing their respect. I couldn't help but think that it was a shame how people would celebrate you in death instead of giving you your flowers when you are still alive to receive them.

Since I no longer knew who to trust, I didn't attend the service. I watched discreetly from a distance, not sure if my enemies were tracking me. After everyone left, I walked over to my mom's tombstone. I knelt down and placed a single red rose over her grave.

"My beautiful mother. Please forgive me. I'm the reason you're dead but I promise, I will find out who did this to you, and they will pay with their life," I vowed, sealing that promise with a kiss on my mother's grave.

Jersey Girl

Three months had passed since I made my escape from Brooklyn, and I was starting to warm up to the idea of becoming a Jersey Girl. I could get used to shopping at upscale malls and living on the water with NYC views. However, living in a hotel on the water was starting to put a dent in my finances, even with my million-dollar come up. I knew it was time for me to lock down a more permanent residence and was doing some brainstorming while I was getting pampered at the nail salon.

While getting a pedicure, the chick in the chair sitting next to me was being extra animated. I had no interest in her conversation until she mentioned rent. At that point I started listening carefully. On the sly I turned to size the girl up. She reminded me of one of those college preppy types, all goody-goody and shit.

Which was cool since I needed a major break from the typical ratchet ass chicks I dealt with.

"Rent is due in less than a week and Crystal had the audacity to move out without giving me any notice. I don't know how I'm going to come up with the money to cover next month's rent," she complained to whoever she was speaking to on the phone.

This might be a win/win, I thought to myself. She needs someone to help pay her rent and I need a more permanent place to stay. Now that my mother was gone, besides occasionally speaking with Bree to stay in the loop, I cut ties with Brooklyn, as I didn't trust anyone. I made the switch to being a Jersey girl, maybe getting a roommate was exactly what I needed. When she ended her call, I decided to shoot my shot. I put on my best All American girl voice and inquired about her apartment.

"Hi, it wasn't my intention to eavesdrop on your conversation, but I heard you mention something about needing a roommate."

I noticed the chick now sizing me up. She eyed all the shopping bags I had next to my chair after what I called therapy splurging. Then she peeped my expensive designer purse with matching shoes, and the diamond tennis bracelet around my wrist. I was giving off rich man's housewife vibes.

"Yes, my roommate bailed on me without any notice. There is no way I can afford the rent on my own. Are you looking for a place to live?"

"Actually, I am. I recently moved to Jersey and I'm staying at a hotel. I was going to start looking for my own place, but it would be great to have a roommate, especially since I don't know anybody here."

"What hotel are you staying at?"

"The W in Hoboken."

"Oh, I know where that is. It's really nice and really expensive," she emphasized.

"Yeah, it is nice and very costly. I can't afford to live in a hotel forever."

"True. Well, I stay in Edgewater. My rent is a little pricey because I live in a high-rise by the Hudson River waterfront."

"How much is the rent?" I asked, knowing whatever the price it would be better than my high ass hotel bill.

"$5000. So, if you took the place your part would be $2500, plus half for utilities. Is that within your budget?"

"Definitely. I'll even pay you six months in advance."

Those magic words had her eyes twinkling and widened in disbelief. I knew it was a done deal at that point. We went from sizing each other up to exchanging smiles.

"I'm Rhonda. It's a pleasure to meet you," she said extending her arm so we could shake hands.

"Precious. It's a pleasure to meet you too, roomie."

Within a week I had moved into Rhonda's high-rise apartment in Edgewater, New Jersey. She lived in a beautiful complex called The Glasshouse. The small city of Edgewater was different than any place I had ever been. It seemed so bright and cheerful, nothing like the projects in Brooklyn. Although only a tunnel and a bridge separated us, I felt like Brooklyn was thousands of miles away.

The apartment was spacious, and the huge windows had beautiful views of New York City and the Hudson River. She also had an expansive private balcony but without that W Hotel panoramic waterfront price. There was smart home technology, just some real fancy shit.

"Welcome home!" Rhonda said excitedly, clinking our glasses. We were sitting on the sofa sharing a bottle of champagne, celebrating being new roommates.

"Thank you! It's nice to be living in an actual apartment, instead of a hotel room."

"I think we're going to have a lot of fun together as roomies."

"Me too."

"I hope you don't mind me asking, but what do you do? You drive a new Benz, you have expensive jewelry, designer clothes, shoes, and you gave me six

months of rent upfront. Money obviously isn't an issue for you."

I took a long sip of champagne debating for a second if I wanted to tell Rhonda the truth. I was getting tired of talking all proper and tying to pretend to be all happy-go-lucky. "My ex was a drug kingpin. I was what you call a hustler's wife. Before he got locked up, he left me a generous sum of money."

"Nice. He must have been some hustler."

"No doubt."

"So, what is he locked up for?"

"Murder."

"Who did he kill?"

"His best friend." Rhonda sat there dumbfounded. She definitely didn't know anything about the streets.

"My life is awfully boring compared to the one you've seemed to live."

She had no idea, I said to myself.

"Enough about me, what do you do?"

"I work at Atomic Records in the marketing department."

"That sounds fun. You must meet mad celebrities."

"Yeah, and unfortunately most of them are demanding and annoying as fuck."

In the midst of laughing, I got distracted when a text message from Inga popped up. I went from having a beaming smile to a grimacing expression on my face.

"Is everything okay?"

"Yeah, it's just a friend I haven't spoken to in a while. She's in town and wants to meet."

"By the look on your face you don't seem too excited to see her."

"I'm not. We used to be close but before I moved to Jersey, she started feeling more like an enemy instead of a friend. She seems to think we have some unresolved issues to discuss," I said right as my phone started vibrating and now it was Inga calling. "Give me a second, I need to take this."

I went outside on the balcony and closed the door.

"What is it, Inga?"

"We need to talk." Her tone was loud and demanding.

"About what?" I hadn't spoken to Inga in almost three months, so her funky attitude was rubbing me the wrong way.

"We can discuss that when I see you."

"No, we can discuss it right now, or you won't be seeing me."

"I don't wanna do this over the phone, Precious. I need to see you face to face."

"On the real, Inga, you sound a lil' hostile, which makes me think this might be some sort of set up. So, I'm not meeting your sneaky ass anywhere."

"Ain't nobody tryna set you up, Precious. No matter what, we still peoples."

"I wanna believe you telling the truth Inga, that we still peoples. We've been best friends for years, but you got me feeling that I need to keep my guard up wit' you."

"I am telling the truth. But I do need to speak to you. I would prefer to do it in person."

"When?"

"Today, if possible."

"A'ight, meet me in the city in an hour. I'll call and let you know the exact location when I get there."

I made sure to be strapped with my Glock when I met up with Inga. I wanted to believe we were still peoples and that our friendship could survive all the bullshit from the last few months, but I didn't trust her. If I got so much as a hint, she was on some shiesty shit to set me up, I was gonna waste her ass, pregnant or not.

When I got to the city, I sent Inga a text and told her to meet me at Central Park in twenty minutes. I was already there, but it would give me an opportunity to observe and see if I saw anybody that looked suspicious.

Inga finally showed up, with her belly proudly poked out. I watched her for ten more minutes, while I finished drinking my white chocolate mocha. I wanted to see if she got on the phone or if she was making eye contact with anyone in the crowd. Once I felt safe, I snuck up behind her.

"What's up, Inga?"

"Oh shit, you scared the fuck outta me, Precious."

"That was the point," I stressed, sitting down on the bench next to her. "Here, I brought your favorite." I handed Inga the drink I got her from Starbucks. "I made sure it was decaffeinated. With you being pregnant I wasn't certain if caffeine was okay for the baby."

"Thanks, I'm surprised you remembered," Inga said instantly devouring her Caramel Frappuccino.

"We've been best friends for years. There's a lot of things I remember. I guess bringing you your favorite drink is my way of showing you that."

"Much appreciated," Inga nodded and then she gave me a slight smile. For a moment I was optimistic there was a real chance we could salvage our friendship.

"So, what was so urgent that you could only discuss it with me face to face?"

"Precious, I need you to be honest wit' me about something."

"OK."

"Were you seeing Ritchie behind my back and were you pregnant by him?"

"Who told you that?"

"That don't matter."

"If you want me to answer your question it does."

"Porsha said that Nico told her you was a snake bitch because you were fucking his best friend behind

his back. He also said you was pregnant by Ritchie and was planning on leaving him so ya could be together."

"Oh, so you talk to Porsha now. You friends wit' my enemy...y'all trauma bondin'?"

"Answer the question, is it true?"

"I was fuckin' Ritchie, but no, I was never pregnant by him, although I told Nico I was."

"Precious, why?" Inga's voice cracked and tears swelled up in her eyes.

"Because after I found out about Porsha, I wanted Nico to suffer. I knew fuckin' his best friend would do the trick."

"But you knew Ritchie was my boyfriend, and we loved each other."

"Inga, wake up! Ritchie didn't give a fuck about you. He begged me to leave Nico, but I neva wanted that clown ass nigga. I told you not to get caught up in his trifling ass, but you swore he was the one," I reminded her, shaking my head. Inga was crushed by what I said, but she asked for the truth.

"That's some foul shit, even for you Precious." Inga's expression reeked of devastation. The tension between us loomed in the air.

"Inga, I never wanted you to get hurt, but Nico had to pay for the pain he caused me. You shouldn't take any of this personally. Ritchie meant nothing to me. He was a means to an end."

"Nico didn't kill Ritchie because he found out he was setting him up. He killed Ritchie because you told him you were fuckin' his best friend...that's what happened isn't it?"

"Why don't you ask Porsha since she seems to be your new source of information."

"I don't need to. You planned all of this. You knew I was pregnant. How could you set up my baby daddy to be killed?"

"Inga, you told me yourself Ritchie said he would cut the baby out of you if you didn't have an abortion. I'm the one that hit you off wit' 50 g's so you could give your baby a start in life. That's more than Ritchie ever did for you or would've done."

"Things might've been different if you stayed out the way. He didn't change until he started fuckin' you. Now Ritchie is dead, and my child will never know his father."

"Well, join the muthafuckin' club 'cause I don't know my daddy neither, and what."

There was an agonizing moment of silence. Inga turned away from me and for a second seemed to get lost in her thoughts while watching some little kids playing on the swings at the park. The afternoon sun was glaring in our path as the wind was blowing the trees in every direction. Adults and children enjoying the beautiful spring day strolled past us. From the idyllic picture, the strangers passing by would've never expected that two former best friends were having a life-changing conversation.

"Was it worth it, just so you could punish Nico for

cheating on you wit' some trick?"

"I've asked myself that very same question, and the answer is yes. Nico disrespected me to the fullest, knowing the streets always be watching. If I had done the same thing to him, he would've sent me home in a body bag."

"Have you ever considered that he still might?"

I cut my eyes at Inga. "Not from behind bars he won't."

"Well, for your sake you better pray that's where he stays. Because if Nico gets out, he won't rest until you're six feet under."

Inga wasn't telling me nothing that I didn't already know. Nico getting out could never be. It was no longer safe for both of us to walk the same streets.

Between my conversation with Inga and Nico's attorney requesting a speedy trial, which meant he would be going to court in the next couple of weeks, my nerves were raw. The high-profile case was drawing all sorts of different opinions from legal experts. Some said he would be found guilty, and many others said the Prosecution's case was weak and Nico would walk. All I thought was *Say It Ain't So*. There was no way Nico could beat the case. If he did, there would be no place on this earth I could hide. He would hunt me down like an animal.

Bad And Boujee

The headline on the front cover of the *"New York Post"* read **Notorious Drug Kingpin Found Guilty of Murder**. Underneath there was a prominent picture of Nico dressed in one of his custom-made designer suits, looking more like a Wall Street businessman than a cold-blooded killer. He was standing at the defense table beside his high-priced attorney handcuffed being escorted out the courtroom. I was finally able to exhale, knowing that Nico would be spending the rest of his life behind bars. After reading the full story, I celebrated by cooking a big breakfast.

"Good morning, Precious," Rhonda said when she entered the kitchen.

"Good morning to you!" I cheered sounding un-usually chipper for this early in the morning.

"Anything good in the paper?" Rhonda asked as

she picked up the New York Post I just put down on the counter.

"What's this?" she questioned, reading the headlines about Nico. "Look at him, he's hot. Who would think someone that fine could be a murderer? Now I know where all the sexy men are...locked up."

I refused to engage in the conversation because I didn't want Rhonda to know that my kingpin and the one on the cover of the Post were one in the same.

"Do you have any plans tonight?" she asked, finally putting the paper down.

"No, why you ask?"

"Atomic Records is having an album release party for Supreme tonight. You're welcome to come."

"Supreme the rapper?"

"Yeah. He's sexy too, right?"

"Fuckin' yes. I didn't know Supreme is on the same label you work for. Love his music, especially the collab he did with Lil Baby. But, nah, I'm not going out tonight. You can bring me back one of those gift bags you always come home with after your events. They be having all sorts of cute items in them."

"Why don't you want to come? It'll be fun."

"I just wanna stay at home tonight, stuff my face with comfort food and watch my all-time favorite movie, Set It Off."

"I hear you but let me know if you change your mind. And don't wait up for me. I won't be home until late."

"Cool, try not to shake yo' ass too hard," I smiled. Part of me did want to go to the party. It would be the perfect way to dance on Nico's prison grave but the other part of me wanted to just stay home and relax.

I'd been feeling uneasy ever since my conversation with Inga at Central Park. Hearing her say Nico would basically hunt me down and kill me if he beat his case made my blood run cold. For the last few weeks, I'd been losing sleep waiting for the trial to end and the verdict to be announced. But even with the guilty verdict, I wasn't completely stress free. For the rest of the day, I pretty much moped around, doing entirely too much thinking, until my phone rang. I hated answering private calls, but I was happy to do anything to get my mind off Nico. "Hello."

"Precious, what's up? You gotta minute?" I immediately recognized Inga's voice and everything inside me wanted to press end. We hadn't spoken to each other since our meeting in the city, and I preferred to keep it that way. Once Inga revealed that her and Porsha were in communication, I wanted nothing to do with her.

"Why you calling me from a private number?"

"I figured you might not answer if you knew it was me and it's important I speak to you."

"All I have is one minute," I said eyeing the clock on the microwave, because I meant that shit.

"Well, then let me get right to it. I need some money." I had to step back from my phone to make

sure I heard Inga correctly.

"Excuse me. Did I hear you right?"

"Yes. You were the only person I knew to call for help."

"Before I even respond, what happened to the 50 g's I gave you less than six months ago?"

"It's gone. I had to buy a car and get some things for me and the baby."

"Inga, the baby ain't even here yet and you spent all the money. What type of car did you buy?"

"That don't matter, Precious. The point is, I don't have no more, and the baby will be here soon. So, I was hoping you could hit me off wit' a hundred thousand."

"I don't have a hundred thousand, and even if I did, I wouldn't give it to yo' simple ass."

"You ain't gotta call me no names, neither. I just figured since you stole that million from Nico, the least you could do was put a hundred thousand in my pocket. I mean you are responsible for making my unborn child fatherless."

With that said, I was tempted to break the promise I made to myself of staying out of Brooklyn, so I could go stomp Inga's ass.

"I don't know where you gettin' your misinformation, but I didn't steal no million dollars from Nico. I'm tryna maintain out in these streets just like you. So whateva you heard, or you think you know is all bullshit. As for your bastard child being fatherless, you gonna have to take the charge on that for being a stupid bitch."

"Precious, you always thought you were better than everybody else and you still do. You walk these streets not thinking about nobody but yourself. But bitch, you can't hide forever.

You think you can break outta Brooklyn and leave everybody behind and forget about all the havoc you caused. You the reason Ritchie is dead, you the reason that Nico is locked up and my instincts tell me you responsible for your mom's death too. But all your scheming is going to come back on you and you gon' take it in blood."

"Suck my dick and lick my balls, Inga! The only blood I'ma take is yours, if you don't leave me the fuck alone," I warned before ending the call. I was getting closer to going over the edge. I immediately threw on my clothes, grabbed my purse and headed out the door.

I found myself doing what I typically do when I'm under stress...go shopping. As I walked through the mall, a sexy red sleeveless slip dress with a plunging neckline hanging in the window of a store caught my eye. At that moment, I decided to go to the album release party tonight and shake my ass with Rhonda.

Never one to be on time, I arrived at the venue when the party was about to end. I'd called Rhonda and told her I was on my way, two hours later I was finally making an appearance. As I was walking towards the entrance, an entourage of people rushed passed

me to an awaiting black Suburban that had what you call limo tinted windows. I glanced to see who it was since there was a frenzied buzz in the air. For a brief moment I felt this magnetic pull and I found myself locking eyes with a strikingly fine ass nigga who I could've sworn was Supreme.

"You need to come in, Miss, there are people waiting behind you," the humongous bouncer demanded, snapping me out of the love connection I had just made.

When I turned back around, the Suburban had driven off. *I guess it wasn't meant to be* I thought to myself.

"Precious, there you are," Rhonda said as she greeted me at the door. "That sure was a long I'm on my way," she cracked.

"My apologies but time is neva on my side."

"It was time well spent," Rhonda commented as she glanced over my outfit. "Love your dress. And your body in it. You that girl," she playfully patted my butt.

"Thank you. It was actually my motivation for coming out tonight. When I saw it at the mall, I was like this dress has been patiently waiting for my arrival," I joked. "But I wish I would've gotten here earlier 'cause it seem like it was real cute event," I said glancing around the posh venue.

"Yeah, it was. All the A-list celebrities we invited came through, but they typically do show up for Supreme."

"Speaking of Supreme, where is the guest of honor?"

"You literally just missed him." Rhonda confirmed what I believed to be true.

Damn, Supreme was the fine ass nigga I made eye contact wit'. I knew there was something familiar about him, I said to myself.

Although Rhonda had invited me to a few industry parties, this was the first one I ever came to. It definitely wasn't like the clubs in Brooklyn. The people in here gave off this aura of being on some real phony Hollywood type-shit. During the time I was there, Rhonda spent half of it giving fake hugs and kisses to a few motherfuckers that she obviously didn't like.

Everyone's favorite departing line was "I'll call you, let's do drinks." Other than that, the music was on point, the spot was sexy, and for the most part, the people were giving off new money but with classy vibes, not that gaudy shit.

After I got a taste of industry parties, I was addicted. Rhonda and I lived on the club scene. It was impossible not to become immersed with partying in those circles. It hit different than clubbing in Brooklyn. And since I had that guap, I kept bottles of champagne flowing at every party we attended. Rhonda would constantly joke with me and say, "Who was your exman? Was he on some New Jack City, Nino Brown type crime boss level?"

I would laugh it off and pop the next bottle. But I

had to watch how I moved and remind myself I wasn't in the grimy streets of Brooklyn anymore. One night when Rhonda and I were leaving a club, some dude pressed up on me. I politely told him to "back off." A few minutes later when we were in the car, I heard a tap on my window, and it was the same dude. I thought it might be someone Nico sent to kidnap or kill me. I reached for my piece and cocked that muthafucka so quick and told the dude I would leave his brains splattered on that concrete if he didn't get the fuck away from me.

I thought the nigga was gonna piss in his pants. All he was trying to do was get my contact info. I overreacted but where I come from, being lax can get you killed. It was funny though, because in a split-second Rhonda's face went from stunned to admiration.

That night we seemed to bond in a more profound way. Something about Rhonda was cool. She wasn't about that life, yet I could tell she would be a loyal friend. With my background, that was a priceless trait to me. She had become like fam, so of course I paid for her to get the ultimate glow up. It wouldn't be fair for me to be the only bad bitch when we hit the clubs together. I'm talking complete transformation, hair, makeup and a new wardrobe. Rhonda was a semi-cute girl, she reminded me of a book smart version of a young Brandy. After we finished her makeover, she blossomed into the well-polished attractive R&B version. Now we were both Bad and Boujee.

Excuse Me Miss

"Aren't you glad you came to this car show with me," Rhonda remarked when we entered the indoor arena. Everywhere you turned there were luxury superlative performance sports cars, motorcycles and the latest and greatest green technology.

"For sure, especially since this is the first time I've ever attended one. They got a DJ and everything. The high energy, music, photographers, exotic cars, all these people, it's giving street party vibes."

"I agree. Unfortunately, this isn't a party for me, I'm here to work. One of our new artists is performing later, so I need to get backstage and make sure every-thing is straight. Will you be okay by yourself?"

"Of course. Go handle yo' business. Come find me once you're done. Fingers crossed by then I would've latched myself to a guy who is easy on the eyes, and I can finesse out some paper," I winked and walked off.

Truth be told, I was hoping to find me a new nigga at this car show. Not to be my man but to fuck. The last time I had some dick was when I fucked Nico the night he killed Ritchie. That was months ago. I was tired of pleasing myself. I was long overdue for a proper pipe down.

All eyes were on me as I parlayed through the crowd. I could hear loud whispers from people trying to figure out who I was. Although I kept it simple, with some fitted jeans, a low-cut white tank top and some open-toe stilettos, my pretty face, body and bling had me looking like I was that girl—bougie, bad, bossy and rich as fuck.

I was led by the music towards a dance battle taking place on the main stage. The freestyle competition had various performers doing krump, waacking, popping, locking and break-dancing. Dudes kept walking up on me trying to engage in conversation, but I was engrossed in the entertainment on the stage, and they were all giving off low vibration, so I acted like they were invisible. That was until a pair of eyes met mine. He was surrounded by security, but a sense of familiarity came over me.

"Excuse me Miss, didn't I see you outside a club about a month or so ago?"

"You're Supreme." I mumbled, sounding like a Stan.

"Yep, that would be me. Aren't you the young lady that was going into the club as I was leaving?"

"Yes, that was me. I can't believe you remember." I felt a big yikes right after I said that, and he had me blushing like a groupie.

"Of course I remember. I'd never forget a face as beautiful as yours."

I never considered myself to be a groupie bitch or a sack chaser. Even with all the hustlers I fucked with, I just wrote that off as me preferring niggas with heavy pockets because I liked expensive things. No doubt I was curious about the lifestyle of the rich and famous, but it wasn't that deep for me because where I came from, I was the superstar. I represented for my borough the same way these so-called celebrities represented for their clique. Their fan base just so happened to reach millions, where mine only reached thousands. But the feeling of being on top was still the same. So, when Supreme was standing in front of me saying how beautiful I was, I wasn't sure if he had me open because he was a famous rapper or because he was fine as fuck. Or maybe it was a combination of both.

"Can you stop making me blush in front of all these people."

"That wasn't my intention. What I wanted was for you to walk with me, talk with me and then hopefully we exchange numbers."

"How about I leave with you, be with you and hopefully chill with you for a very long time."

In the midst of me trying to finesse this nigga,

Rhonda popped up and gave Supreme a hug.

"What's up, Supreme!"

"What's good, Rhonda," Supreme said with ease, then turning his attention back to me. "Just so you know, I work with her—that's it."

"Supreme, she's my roommate. You don't have to explain yourself," Rhonda laughed.

"You live together? Damn Rhonda, you never told me you had all that at home." Supreme extended his hand towards me like he was presenting me as a grand prize.

"She came to your album release party, but I think you had already left."

"Yeah, we made eye contact on my way out. Then I was blessed to see her once again today. Damn, I didn't even get your name."

"Precious."

"That name fits you perfectly. So, are you gonna walk with me or what?" Supreme asked. He had this silky yet commanding voice. It was hard to explain but it only added to his sex appeal.

"That depends. Are you going to leave with me, be with me and chill with me?"

"You didn't even have to ask that twice. I heard you the first time and the answer is, I wouldn't have it any other way."

With that I took Supreme's hand beaming like a little girl with her first adolescent crush. I waved bye to Rhonda and Supreme and I walked off, with his security guards surrounding us. We spent the duration of the car show together like I was his date. That night, all of us, including Rhonda, went out for dinner and drinks. Afterwards, instead of staying in the room with Rhonda, I went with Supreme to his hotel suite. I was ready to put an end to the sex drought I had been on.

Once I took a shower, I laid in the bed next to Supreme ready to do all sorts of tricks with my tongue.

"I enjoyed spending the day with you and then all of us going out for dinner. It was really nice," I said easing closer to him.

"I enjoyed myself too."

"The fun doesn't have to stop now." I began sprinkling kisses on Supreme's neck.

"Precious, I just want you to fall asleep in my arms."

"I can do that right after we fuck."

"Baby, I don't want to fuck you."

"What you mean you don't want to fuck me? What...is there something wrong wit' me?" I asked becoming defensive, moving away from Supreme, and covering my body with the bedsheet. I was drowning with embarrassment.

"Look at me." Supreme put his hand on my face. "Physically, you're perfect. And I want you in every way. When we become intimate, I don't want us to fuck. I want us to make love. There's a difference. I'm genuinely feeling you. I felt this sort of connection to you in just that brief moment we locked eyes in front

of the club. You're special and I want our relationship to reflect that. That means not giving into lust but getting to know each other and appreciating what's on the inside. Will you do that with me? Take our time so we can build something real?"

I stared into Supreme's dark mysterious eyes. I was filled with confusion. No man had ever asked to get to know me as a person before. When I was ready to fuck, till we see the sun, so were they. Yet, here was this rap superstar, who probably had mad bad bitches begging to take their turn and ride his dick, telling me that he wanted us to wait and get to know each other better first. His request seemed so pure and once his words sunk it, it was frightening yet intriguing to me.

"Yes, I want to build something real with you also," I said, snuggling underneath his arms and falling asleep next to his warm body.

The last few weeks of spending time with Supreme had proven to be rousing. When we weren't together, he stayed on my mind constantly. The nigga had me straight tripping. He didn't want no ass, just conversation. The funny thing was I never felt closer to any man in my life. With all the talking we did; I got past the initial physical attraction and grew to know the man. From listening to the lyrics in his music and watching his videos, I would have never guessed that Supreme was this kind, romantic gentleman. While we were sitting on the blanket at the park with our picnic basket, sharing fresh fruit, and taking turns feeding each other strawberries, I felt like the luckiest girl in the world.

"The last few weeks have been unbelievable. You're the most amazing man I've ever known, Supreme."

"You make it easy. I enjoy being around you. I feel relaxed, at ease. It doesn't hurt that you're easy on the eyes too," he smiled. "Who do you resemble, your mother or your father?"

"I would have to say my mother."

"I'm looking forward to meeting her. I want to thank the woman that gave birth to such a gorgeous daughter. She has to be special."

"Unfortunately, that'll never happen."

"Why? Are the two of you not on good terms?"

"We ain't on no terms. My mother is dead." I stated abruptly.

"What? I'm sorry. How long has she been gone?"

"About seven months."

"Man, that's recent. How did she die?"

I pushed the bowl of fruit away. Supreme's question triggered all these emotions that I preferred to keep buried. I put my head down to hide the tears swelling in my eyes.

"My mother was murdered and before you come asking me about my daddy, 'cause I know that's next;

I don't know who he is. I ain't never met my dad. My mother sold her body for drugs, she probably didn't know who my father was."

"Baby, I didn't mean to upset you." Supreme gently stroked my arm, trying to soothe my broken spirit.

"It's not your fault. How were you supposed to know that I came from nothing."

"Don't ever say that about yourself. You did come from something. You don't realize how special you are. But if you let me, I'll show you. I want to give you the world."

Supreme leaned in close to kiss me. In that instant he turned my pain into butterflies.

Why Don't We Fall In Love

I freed the last roller in my hair, giving my silk press that big, beautiful voluminous visual I was going for. It hit just right with the strapless, multi-colored mesh dress I was wearing. I dabbed on a little more Fenty Gloss Bomb and was ready to go.

When I walked in the living room Rhonda was still laying on the couch watching television, with a heating pad on her stomach. There was a cup of herbal tea and a bottle of pain medicine on the table next to her.

"It sucks you're sick and can't come with me to Supreme's show tonight."

"I know. But these cramps are kicking my ass. You have to count me out."

"I hate I'm rolling solo."

"It's probably for the best. Maybe you'll finally get some."

"Right!" I smacked. "Can you believe I've been seeing this dude for two months and we still haven't fucked? But you know what's really bothering me, Rhonda?"

"What?"

"I know he's fucking somebody."

"Why you say that?"

"Sweetheart, ain't no nigga voluntarily giving up pussy, especially when it's new. It ain't like there's a drought out here either, especially not for a man like Supreme. I haven't figured out whether I should be flattered or offended that he's not fucking me."

"Damn, Precious, I don't know how you're able to be around a man as fine as Supreme and not get none."

"Who you telling? All this let's get to know each other first initially had me intrigued. And I have to admit, Supreme's approach did work because I have genuine feelings for him and it's a little scary. I find myself lying in the bed staring at a picture we took together, just missing him all the time. That's a clear indication to me that he might have me open," I confessed.

"If Supreme is giving you that bubbly feeling in the pit of your stomach, I heard that's what happens when you're falling in love."

"Let's slow down, Rhonda. What I need to handle right now is convincing Supreme to cut all this foreplay, which in our case, is the hours on the phone talking, and dinner dates. It's time to get straight to the dessert."

"I'm assuming dessert is sex, and that sounds like a good plan, but you better hurry up, or you're going to miss the concert."

I glanced down at my watch. "You're right. I have to go. Luckily, if I miss the show, there's always the afterparty," I winked and headed out.

"Have fun!" Rhonda called out before the door closed shut.

Of course, after running my mouth off to Rhonda, I was late and missed Supreme's show. Luckily, I had the details for the afterparty and went straight to the hotel. When I arrived at the penthouse suite there was wall-to-wall people, drinking, smoking, dancing and mingling. I weaved through the crowd looking for Supreme. I spotted him in a private area sitting on the couch, with a bottle of champagne on the table. To my disgust, he was fully engaged in a conversation with what looked like an Instagram hoochie. She was smiling and giggling while sipping champagne from her glass.

"Oh, so I guess you found someone to keep you company huh, Supreme?"

"Precious, you finally made it. I waited for you backstage, but you never came."

"So, what you scooped up the first piece of ass you could to replace me?"

"Excuse me!" the hoochie barked obviously offended.

"Bitch, you heard what the fuck I said. Why don't you sit there like a good mutt and mind yo' business. This here is between me and Supreme."

"Listen, I don't know who you think you are, but..." Supreme put his hand out to stop her from completing her sentence. I guess he called himself deescalating the situation before we started to throw hands.

"I apologize. Precious is a very close friend of mine, and she is misreading what's going on between us, which for the record is nothing," Supreme explained sounding all diplomatic and shit.

"Fuck you, Supreme. I knew you were full of shit. Is this why you don't fuck me 'cause you stickin' your dick in other bitches. You stay here and entertain this chick. I'm out."

I bolted before I picked up that bottle and busted it upside Supreme's head. I was furious because I should've never let myself get open off him. I certainly didn't think I would ever let a nigga love bomb me. Supreme had me crashing out in front of random broads like I was a goofy bitch.

I was swerving back through the crowd as different men were trying to get my attention. Some even had the nerves to grab my hand. I kept pushing them away until my gaze became fixated on a cutie leaning against the wall. I responded to the lust in his eyes and walked directly in his path. Without exchanging words, we began tonguing each other down. In that moment I wanted to forget how Supreme made me feel like a sucker. This was my way of saying fuck you.

"Yo, what the fuck are you doing!" Supreme yanked me from the man's embrace and pushed me against the wall.

"Supreme, man this yo' girl? I had no idea." The guy put his hands up, being extra apologetic.

"No, I'm not his girl, just his close friend."

"Yeah, this my girl," Supreme shot back, tightening his grip on me.

"That's not what you called me when you were gettin' all cozy on the couch wit' that chick."

"Yo, shut the fuck up!"

"Man, I'm sorry. I didn't know that was your girl. No disrespect."

The guy was still apologizing when two huge bodyguards came marching towards us, ready to toss him out the party.

"Everything's cool." Supreme put his hand up, stopping the security. He then directed his attention back to the guy. "But you can go now," he said brushing him off.

Supreme grabbed me by my wrist and lead me down to the end of the hallway until we got to a closed

door. He pulled me into a bedroom and slammed the door.

"What the fuck is wrong with you?"

"What the fuck is wrong wit' me? What about you! Carrying on wit' that bitch!"

"We were talking, that's it. If you got to the show on time and met me backstage like you were supposed to, then I wouldn't have been talking to anybody else."

"Now it's my fault you were cozying up wit' the next chick. I guess it's my fault too that you don't want to have sex wit' me."

"Is that what this is about? You want me to fuck you, is that what you want Precious? Hum, answer me." Supreme grabbed at me roughly. He began tugging at my dress, putting his hands around my waist and pressing my hips against him. "Oh, now you don't have nothing to say. Either you want me to fuck you, or you don't. Which one is it?"

I was silent, shocked by Supreme's aggressive behavior but completely turned on. He put his hands up my dress and ripped off my panties.

"How do you want me to fuck you, Precious, from the front or from the back?" Supreme pinned my arms against the wall, forcing me to look at him in the eyes. "How do you want me to fuck you? Answer me!"

The next thing I knew, Supreme had me bent over a chair pounding my pussy out. My ass jiggled against his dick with each thrust.

"Oh, Supreme, baby you feel so good," I moaned.

"You was going to give all this ass to some nigga you didn't even know."

"No, baby, I was just tryna make you jealous."

"Don't lie to me."

"I swear, I only want you."

"You better 'cause this pussy is mine now. If you ever try some trifling shit like that again, I will fuck you up. You understand me?"

"Yes."

"You sure?"

"Yes, it won't neva happen again." That night I got the best dick down of my life. Now I understood why Supreme wanted to wait, because he knew once he put it on me, I would be officially sprung.

Mortal Combat

Some good dick can do wonders for a bitch. Now that Supreme was slaying me on a regular basis, I didn't have a care in the world. I was acting all giddy for the nigga and I loved every minute of it.

Rhonda instantly knew when I got some because she said my face kept a glow. But it was more than just sex for me. I knew Supreme also had my mind because I got butterflies in my stomach every time my phone would ring hoping it was him. Going through withdrawals when I went to sleep without him by my side. Scared that a bitch with a prettier face, bigger tits and ass might catch his eye and steal him away. Those were always some of the telltale signs that I heard so many girls speak of but never thought it would happen to me. I guess that meant I was in love or deeply infatuated. For that reason, I temporarily buried any insecurities or fear of being hurt and allowed myself to enjoy the ride. Anytime I had an opportunity to spend time with Supreme, I was all in.

So, when he asked me to come to the city and meet him at the studio, I couldn't get there fast enough. When I was halfway over the George Washington Bridge, I realized I was running mad early. With plenty of time to spare, I stopped by my old apartment on Riverside Drive. It'd been months since I checked on the spot. I had even considered sub-leasing it, since Inga wasn't staying there, but I didn't need the money. Plus, I liked knowing that I always had a place to crash, if need be.

Although this apartment building didn't have all the luxury amenities of my place in Jersey, I somewhat missed living here. It was my very first apartment, so it held a lot of sentimental value. There was a tad bit of nostalgia taking the elevator up to the seventh floor. When I stepped off, I immediately heard loud music. When I lived here, I remembered it being eerily quiet, so I was surprised. Everyone on my floor was either old or married with young children. When I got closer to my door, I realized the music was coming from my apartment. I put the key in the lock and when I tried to open it, the chain blocked any further entrance. I heard a female voice scream over the music, "Is that you, Inga?"

"Hun, hmmm," I grumbled loudly. *I know Inga's trifling ass is not staying here. That bitch told me she*

*was staying in Brooklyn at her mom's crib. But who
the fuck is in there, Inga ain't got no sister,* I thought to
myself.

I unzipped my purse and pulled out my gun
but put it back and decided to get my knife instead.
I stepped away from the door so I wouldn't be seen
through the peephole. Once I heard the chain released,
I grabbed the knob and forcibly pushed the door
open. The door knocked the girl in the head, and she
screamed out in pain covering her face. Without missing a beat, I slammed the door shut and jumped on top
of the girl, pinned her arms down with my knees and
put the knife to her neck. When I saw who it was, my
first instinct was to slit her throat, but I needed to get
some answers first.

"Porsha, what the fuck are you doing in my
apartment?"

"I knew I should've had those locks changed."

"Bitch, you got bigger problems than that right
now. How long has Inga been letting you stay in my
crib?"

Porsha rolled her eyes and remained silent. I had
to remind this heffa she was in my shit, and I was the
shot caller. I put the tip of my knife to her throat and
nipped it deep enough to draw blood. Porsha let out
an involuntary scream. I quickly covered her mouth
with my hand.

"Listen to me, you two-dollar whore. I have no
problem ending your life right now. So, you can either

answer my fuckin' questions or get ready to die." Porsha began to cry like a baby who needed their dirty diaper changed.

"What do you want to know?" Porsha managed to say under sniffles.

"Start by telling me how long Inga been letting you stay here."

"A few months."

"Why would yo' dumbass want to lay up in my spot when you know I can't stand your muthafuckin' ass?"

"It was Nico's idea. He wanted me to stop through to see if you stashed his million dollars here. Then he told me to ask Inga if I could stay here for a while, just in case you came through."

"Well bitch, I'm here now, what you supposed to do?"

"Nico had his boys stationed out front, waiting for you to show up, ready to do whatever to get his money. After a while, we decided you was ghost and not coming back. But I like having my own place, so I decided to stay."

"When you say Nico told his boys to do whatever in order to get his money, you mean kill me?"

"No, that was the one thing he instructed them not to do. He said killing you was a pleasure he was saving for himself."

"Why does Nico believe I have his money?"

"Tommy was the only one who knew Nico had

the money at his townhouse. One of Nico's street informants told him that after he got locked up, Tommy tried to cross him and went to his crib to steal the million but it was gone. Tommy dead behind that shit too. And when Inga told me the night Ritchie got killed, you stopped by her hotel room and gave her fifty-thousand, Nico said that shit was no coincidence."

"Answer me this, did Nico have my mother killed?" I always thought Nico had one of his workers kill my mother, but I could never explain how they got in her apartment. The door wasn't kicked in and the lock wasn't broken, so whoever did it, my mother let them in. That didn't make sense to me because of the lifestyle my mother lived, she wouldn't open the door for nobody unless she knew you and was expecting you. Anybody else would've had to kick in the door to get to her.

"I don't know if you ready for this, Precious."

"If I asked the question, then it means I'm ready for the answer."

"Nico's street informant was Inga. Her and Tommy was cool, and he told her about the million dollars missing. Inga told Tommy you might've stashed the money at your mom's crib. She knew your mother would open the door for her. Tommy agreed to hit Inga off with seventy-five thousand. All she had to do was let him in your mother's apartment."

I couldn't believe what Porsha was telling me, but it all made sense. Inga felt betrayed about that sorry-ass nigga Ritchie, but to let Tommy kill my mother was the lowest you could go. Inga knew as much hell my mother put me through, she was all I had my entire life. To take her away from me was stealing my last breath.

"Did Inga know Tommy planned on killing my mom?"

"She figured he would but said yo' moms was a crackhead hoe anyway, and him killing her would put her out her misery."

"How could Inga do that to my mother?" I asked myself out loud, shaking my head.

"Precious, real talk Inga blames you for her fucked up life. She believes you messed up her relationship with Ritchie and the reason Nico killed him, leaving her without a father for her son. She's barely surviving and her mother the one that has to babysit her son while she at work."

"She went through the fifty thousand I gave her?"

"Yep. She bought a car, clothes, jewelry and shit."

"Why don't she sell her fuckin' car?"

"She totaled it in an accident and her dumb ass had let the car insurance lapse."

"Call Inga now. Do exactly as I say and don't fuck this up Porsha, or I'll slit your throat," I threatened before handing Porsha the phone while keeping the knife steady at her neck.

Porsha nodded her head agreeing to my demands. I wanted to instill fear in her to the point that she would do as I said. It's not like I cared whether the bitch lived or died, but I did want her to deliver Inga to me.

"Now what?" she asked after calling Inga.

"Let's go. It's time for us to take a ride."

My gun remained pointed directly at Porsha as she drove us to Brooklyn. During our ride, I kept imagining how my mother must've felt when she realized Inga had set her up. Your daughter's so-called best friend bringing death to your front door.

When Porsha pulled up to the projects Inga lived in, I scanned the area looking for where I wanted her to park. "Drive around to that back parking lot. It's always isolated."

"What's next?" an exasperated Porsha questioned once she parked the car. Before I could respond, I got distracted when my phone rang. It was Supreme. *Fuck! I totally forgot I was supposed to meet him at the studio,* I thought to myself ignoring his call. I put my phone on silent as I needed to focus all my attention on dealing with my best friend turned opp.

"Text Inga and let her know you're here." I watched carefully making sure Porsha didn't try no slick shit. Once that was done, we headed to the spot Inga told Porsha to meet her. By this time the sun had went down and darkness was setting in.

While we were standing under the stairwell, I noticed I had two missed calls from Supreme and several text messages. I was tempted to respond but then me and Porsha turned around simultaneously when we heard footsteps approaching. I nodded my head at Porsha, gesturing her to speak up. I then moved behind a brick wall, so I was out of sight as I waited for Inga to get closer.

"Inga, is that you?"

"Who else would it be?" she asked sarcastically. "I knew this would be the perfect place for us to meet. Don't nobody be over here. Now where the money at?"

"In the trunk. I didn't feel comfortable toting around all that cash."

"I feel you. Is Precious' dead body in the trunk too? I don't want her stench fuckin' up our paper," Inga laughed.

"Nah, it's still at the apartment. I need your help moving her body. Dead weight is heavy."

"Yo, I'm so fuckin' happy that bitch is dead, whatever help you need, I got you. I just wish it was me who murked that scandalous hoe."

"Well, here's your opportunity." I stepped from behind the brick wall to what appeared to be a dumbfounded Inga. "Don't stop runnin' your mouth now. Keep poppin' that shit, Inga."

"You trifling bitch! You set me up!" Panic flooded Inga's face, turning her rage on Porsha.

"I ain't have no choice. She was gonna kill me if I didn't get you out here," Porsha griped.

"Both of you trauma bondin' hoes, go stand over

there." I pointed my gun in the direction I wanted them to move.

"Precious, I don't know what Porsha told you, but it's all lies."

"Save it, Inga. I just heard you celebrating and dancing on my grave before I was even buried. But I could even let that go. What I can't let go, is that you set my mother up to die at the hands of Tommy. "

Inga glared at Porsha with pure hate.

"Don't look at me." Porsha crossed her arms and rolled her eyes.

"I didn't know Tommy was gonna kill your mom. I thought he was there to try and find the million dollars. I swear."

"You lying bitch. Porsha, repeat what you said Inga told you about my mother."

"She said your moms was a crackhead hoe anyway and Tommy killing her would put her out of her misery. That's what the fuck you said, Inga," Porsha smacked not backing down.

"You know what's so foul about that, when my mother opened the door to let you in, you knew she was clean. She hadn't used drugs in two months. I saw her the day before she died, and she was more beautiful than ever. But you didn't care. All you wanted was yo' funky seventy-five thousand dollars. But here's what I'll do for you. I'll give that money to your mother to help take care of your son. Think of it as her cashing in on your life insurance policy."

"Precious, I'm so sorry. Please don't kill me. I was just hurt over the whole Ritchie situation. I fucked up, but we can get past this." Inga began sobbing and begging for her life.

"I think this is my cue to go. But like we discussed, Precious, nothing happened. All this stays between me and you."

"Sorry, Porsha. I had a change of heart. All of this stays with me, not you."

Before Porsha could even plea for her life, I aimed the gun right in the center where her mouth dropped when she heard the news and pulled the trigger. The bullet damn near ripped half her head off. "You know I neva liked that bitch."

Inga stared down at Porsha's dead body in horror. She got on her knees and began begging for mercy, although she showed none to my mother.

"Please Precious, it's not too late. We can start all over, get the fuck out of Brooklyn, you, me, and little Ritchie," Inga cried as tears streamed down her face.

"Tell me you didn't name your son after a nigga who didn't give a fuck about you or his seed. You really are too stupid to live."

With that, I put two bullets in Inga. One for the death of my mother, the other for being a stupid cunt and naming her son after his trifling father. I left the two dead snakes lying beside one another. Neither one of them bitches would be having an open casket at their funeral.

Love Is Colder Than Death

Supreme was still furious with me and it was fuckin' my head up. When I didn't show up to the studio, answer his calls or respond to his text messages, he was worried and reached out to Rhonda believing something terrible happened to me. When I finally called him, my brain kept freezing. I couldn't come up with a reasonable explanation why I disappeared for all those hours. He kept telling me to be honest and just admit the truth. But I couldn't seem to come up with a way to say I was out committing two murders. That's when Supreme said he didn't want to speak to me until I was honest with him. I doubted I'd ever be able to tell him the truth as I was still processing it myself. I had killed before, but I couldn't get murdering Inga out of my head.

A week after Inga's funeral, I kept my word and made sure her mother got a hundred thousand dollars for the care of little Ritchie. I gave an extra twenty-five thousand for my guilt. However justified I felt, I was responsible for him growing up not ever knowing his mother or father. The least I could do was give some money to hopefully help the boy have a chance at a future. Inga's mom was always a hard worker and good woman. She wouldn't go blow all the cash on material shit. She would make sure the baby was provided for.

Now here it was weeks later, and I had put Inga's murder behind me but there was still no Supreme. I was becoming restless. My days were getting longer and my nights shorter. I wasn't doing nothing with myself besides lying in bed consumed with sadness. I glanced over at my nightstand ready to finish off my second glass of wine.

"Girl, get out of bed," Rhonda came in my room and said.

"Why?"

"Because you have to stop being depressed over this break you and Supreme are taking. Let's go out and have some drinks or something."

"I'm not up to it. Plus, I already have a drink," I sighed eyeing my glass of wine.

"Do you think Supreme is laying around in his bed mourning you?"

"I'm not mourning Supreme, but I guess being on the outs with him is bothering me more than I wanted

to admit."

Rhonda sat down next to me. "Help me understand. Why didn't you just tell Supreme where you were that day? I mean he was genuinely worried about you."

I sat up in bed and took a sip of wine. *It's a little difficult to explain you can't make it to the studio because you're in Brooklyn killing your former best friend and the hoe who fucked your ex-man that you setup and is now in prison for life,* I thought to myself.

"It's complicated," I chose to say instead.

"So, Supreme is completely ghosting you?"

"Yep. I wish he would get over it. I swore to him I wasn't with another dude or anything. An unexpected emergency that needed to be handled came up," I insisted, which was true. "I wanna believe that Supreme will get over this, but he's so fuckin' stubborn. What if he never comes back."

"Staying cooped up in your bedroom isn't going to make him come back any sooner. I suggest you snap out of this funk you're in." Rhonda pulled the blankets off of me. "Get dressed, we're going to the city to get turnt up!"

That night I reluctantly went with Rhonda to this new upscale lounge in the city. It had the typical crowd of models, actors, social media influencers, music executives and niggas with big bankroll. The place was sexy. It had a modern luxury feel with plush beds scattered throughout the lounge, and a bar designed to look like a block of ice. The hostess sat us in a corner next to some industry heads that Rhonda was cool with. She was mingling over in their bed.

When the waitress brought over our bottle, I sat there sipping my champagne, wishing I could crawl back in my own real bed. I was in no mood to be out and about, but to my devastation, Supreme was. I couldn't help but notice when he walked in with some chick draped on his arm with his bodyguards trailing behind him. They sat on a bed on the other side of the room but still within my view.

Seeing Supreme with that girl felt like someone stabbed me in the heart, twisted it and then left the shit on automatic rotation. The pain cut deep.

"Precious, are you okay? You have this expression on your face like you're stuck in a nightmare."

"That sounds about right. I guess you didn't see Supreme walk in?"

"No, where is he?" Rhonda started looking around.

"Right over there." Rhonda followed my eyes, and we watched as Supreme appeared to be in a deep conversation with his date.

"I told you not to be sitting around mourning over Supreme's ass. You better do a trade-in because

you don't need him. After seeing this, maybe you'll snap out of that coma you've been in for the last few weeks," Rhonda smacked.

I glanced over at Rhonda. I had to make sure I was hearing what I thought I heard. She was advising me on how to move when you lose a nigga. Once that sunk in, the fire that used to burn inside of me suddenly reignited.

"I can't believe you're the one boosting me up. I really do need to get my shit together."

"Finally, you're speaking the right language. If Supreme is keeping himself entertained, maybe you need to do the same."

Rhonda's advice had me on some fuck niggas get money type shit. Then the lyrics to *Wanna Be* started playing in my head and I heard GloRilla and Megan Thee Stallion chanting: ***He don't wanna be saved, don't save him. That is not my nigga, don't claim him. He don't wanna be kept, don't keep him. I don't get left, I'm a leaver...***

Fuck Supreme!! I zoomed in on this flashy guy popping champagne bottles who had been eyeing me since I sat down.

"Do you know who that is?" I nudged Rhonda and discreetly pointed in his direction, then turned away.

"Of course. That's Pretty Boy Mike. He owns Pristine Records. Don't look now but he's on his way over here," Rhonda alerted me.

"You mind if I sit on your bed?"

"Nah, have a seat."

"I know you seen me watching you since you stepped up in here. I didn't think you were interested until I noticed you point me out to your friend."

"Damn, you saw that. I was trying to be discreet, guess it didn't work."

"You acknowledging me, gave me the confidence to come over here and introduce myself. I'm Mike and your name is?" he extended his hand and when I reached out to shake it, he kissed my hand. Pretty Boy Mike had model looks but with a rugged and dangerous edge.

"Nice to meet you, Mike. My name is Precious."

"The pleasure is mine. Do you live in the city?"

"No. I rep Brooklyn, but I live in Jersey now."

"Brooklyn girl. What part of Brooklyn are you from?

"I used to live over there in Riverdale Towers."

"That's hard knock. You so damn gorgeous, I would've never guessed. I got distracted and didn't pay attention to the darkness in your eyes."

"Don't let the face, clothes and jewelry fool you. I'm BK to the fullest," I bragged.

"You know what, Precious, I believe you. A man has to be on top of his game to deal with you. I live in Jersey also, but I too come from the school of hard knocks. I've been around these fake acting Hollywood characters for so long that I'm slipping. I couldn't even

recognize one of my own." Pretty Boy Mike placed his hand on my cheek, and gently rubbed the side of my face. "You my type of girl, beautiful on the outside but if someone bark, you bite back."

Mike had this appeal that made me give him my full attention. To the point, that I didn't even notice Supreme approaching. It seemed like he appeared out of nowhere, standing in front of our bed.

"Precious, I need to speak to you." I took a few seconds to focus on Supreme.

"What up Supreme." Mike reached out his hand but then quickly put it down when Supreme made it clear he would not be showing any love.

"What do you want, Supreme?"

"To speak to you in private."

"Whatever you have to say, you can say it right here."

"You wanna act cute, that's cool. What the fuck are you doing over here wit' this nigga?" Supreme barked.

"Man, there's no need for you to get all hostile. Relax," Mike suggested. Supreme turned to face Pretty Boy Mike.

"This ain't none of yo' business. I'm having a conversation wit' my girl."

"Your girl?" I gave Supreme the why don't you burn face. "That's hard to tell when you came in here wit' some other chick," I reminded him.

"Is that why you letting this nigga touch all on

your face 'cause you seen me with a female? That's not acceptable. Get yo' shit, and let's go."

"I'm not going anywhere with you. You not answering my calls, you been lounging on the bed with the next bitch ever since you came in parading her around. Now you tryna dictate what the fuck I'm supposed to do. Kiss my ass. I'm staying right where the fuck I'm at."

Supreme reached down and grabbed my arm. He tried to pull me from the bed. Mike stepped in and pushed Supreme out the way. From there straight chaos erupted. Supreme's bodyguards swarmed in and attacked Mike. Then the group of guys that came with Mike ran over and started busting bottles over the bodyguard's heads. With all the commotion going on, Supreme grabbed my arm and practically dragged me out the lounge, cussing at me the whole time. We hopped in the back of the chauffeur driven SUV. I pushed Supreme's hand off of me as his driver pulled off.

"What happened to the little armpiece you came with?"

"When I spotted you with that nigga Mike, I knew it was about to be a problem, so I had an Uber pick her up."

"How considerate of you. Who is she supposed to be, your new girlfriend?"

"No, just someone who was keeping me company while my girlfriend was supposed to be getting her

mind right. But instead, you was up in that lounge letting some industry nigga rub all on your face."

"You're the one that's been giving me straight shade for the last few weeks. Do you know how sick I was when I saw you come in there with that girl. It felt like someone stabbed me in the heart."

"When you wouldn't tell me what was going on with you, I was tempted to cut you off. But when I saw you with Mike, I lost it. The thought of you being wit' another nigga was about to make me go ballistic. We gotta find a way to work this shit out 'cause I can't give you up."

"Then don't," I said laying my head on Supreme's shoulder. We intertwined our fingers, locking them together for the duration of the ride.

When we arrived at Supreme's place, the first thing I did was unzip his jeans and put his dick in my mouth. I wanted to taste him so bad, and I also wanted him to remember what my lips felt like wrapped around his manhood. I was in love with Supreme, and I didn't ever want to worry again if he would leave me and never come back.

The Messenger

I never considered myself being capable of falling in love until I would wake up yearning for a taste of Supreme whenever he wasn't next to me. If I was being honest, I knew we were perfect for each other after our first kiss. But I was afraid and kept saying, please don't be too good to be true. The love I felt for him was becoming so strong, that I considered him to be the man I wanted to spend the rest of my life with. Because of that, I debated if it was time for me to tell Supreme about my past.

Of course, not tell him everything, but enough for him to get a general idea about who I am. Or maybe who I was. Falling in love was beginning to soften my heart and make me want to change my ways. All my life, the only person I could depend on was me. Nobody had my back or gave a fuck about me. Everybody

was out for self, including me. It was different now; everything had changed. I knew that Supreme was in love with me like I was in love with him. For the first time somebody valued my life and genuinely cared what happened to me.

As I was getting dressed to meet Supreme in the city, I continued to wrangle with the "should I" or "shouldn't I" do a full confessional with him tonight. I still hadn't made up my mind, but what I did know was unlike last time, I would be showing up at the studio. He was having a session, and I was determined to be on time. We were finally back on track, and I wasn't going to do anything to jeopardize that.

When I turned on 54th street, there was a Mercedes Maybach SUV, a couple G-wagons, Range Rovers and even a Lamborghini parked in front of the studio and lined on the side of the street. It looked more like a car show then a place of business."

"Hi, I'm here to see Supreme."

"Your name?"

"Precious."

"Hold on one moment." The guy got on the phone, and I assumed he was calling the studio to make sure it was OK for me to go in the session. "Sign in and go right through those doors, he's in studio A."

I followed the guy's directions and came to the entry that had the letter A. When I opened the heavy wood door, I walked into a lounge. I stayed on course following the loud music, which led me to the actual studio. The lights were dim, but I could see somebody in the vocal booth messing with his headphones. The guy didn't look like Supreme, though. Then a couple of guys that were hauled up in the corner smoking weed noticed me.

"Who you lookin' for Mami?"

"Supreme. Is this his session?"

"Nah, this the wrong studio."

"Is this studio A?"

"Yeah, but I believe Supreme in studio B. It's right across the hall," he pointed his blunt in that direction.

"Thanks. Sorry about that."

"No problem. You more than welcome to stay."

"Maybe another time." I kept it short but polite. When I turned to exit, there was Pretty Boy Mike standing in my way.

"Precious Cummings. I was hoping to run into you again. I didn't think it would be so soon though."

"Well, here I am. I'm glad we ran into each other too. I wanted to apologize for what happened the other night."

"No need to apologize. It wasn't your fault."

"Appreciate that. I better be going." Mike blocked my path which made it impossible for me to exit.

"You here to see Supreme?"

"Yep. The receptionist sent me to the wrong studio."

"I'll walk you out."

"No need. If you can move out my way, that'll be good."

"But I wanted to talk to you about a mutual friend of ours."

"You must be mistaken 'cause we don't have any mutual friends. I also don't recall giving you my last name."

"I could've sworn you Nico Carter's woman."

Caught off guard, I struggled to come up with some sort of quick denial. I was stunned that out of all the people in the state of New York, our mutual friend had to be my worst enemy.

"I'm Supreme's woman. Nico is my ex."

"Have a seat, Precious. We should talk." Mike moved out my way to take a seat on one of the couches in the lounge area.

"I don't have time. Supreme is waiting for me." I brushed past him dismissively.

"Make time because I have a message for you." Mike's tone was that of a demand not a request. With reluctance I sat down.

"Can you get to it, because like I said, Supreme is waiting for me, so I don't have much time." I made sure Mike could hear the impatience in my voice.

"This won't take long."

"Then spit it out, so I can go." Mike moved close

to me on the couch. I shifted the position of my body as it felt like he was invading my space.

"Before I got involved in the music industry, like Nico, I was also a drug kingpin, which means I still have close ties to people in the game. When I learned about his unfortunate incarceration, I was concerned. As you know, Nico garners a great deal of respect in these streets. When word got out that you were the reason for his predicament, that was a problem."

"I don't know what you're talking about. Nico's incarceration has nothing to do with me!" I pushed back at Mike's accusations.

"The only reason you're still alive, is because at his request, everyone agreed to let him handle you personally. I know firsthand when you're in the game, there's always casualties. People have to die. Sometimes even someone you have love for. So, when Nico gets out, he will end your life. That is my message to you."

"Lucky for me, Nico will be in prison for the rest of his life. Let me ask you a question, Mike. Did you know all this before you was all up in my face, stroking my cheek the other night," I cracked.

"I sincerely admire that fire in you, Precious. You're still a baby and yet you're already a legend in Brooklyn. A true survivor, but unfortunately, it won't keep you alive. Again, I'm just the messenger giving you a warning."

"You mean a death sentence."

"I know Nico taught you the code of the streets. You didn't honestly believe you could walk away from him unscathed. There's always a price to pay for betrayal and disloyalty. It usually means death."

"Are we finished?"

"Yes, we're done here. "

"Good. Fuck you and Nico. And by the way, next time you speak to him, deliver a message on my behalf. Tell Nico I hope he rots in jail for the remainder of his fuckin' life." I stated boldly exiting out.

My heart was racing. I didn't want Mike to know it, but what he said left me paralyzed in fear. I reached a point in my life where I had a reason to live, and here he was, delivering the news that death was right around the corner. My hands were shaking, and I was visibly upset. I didn't want to go in Supreme's session looking so distraught. I stopped in the bathroom and splashed water on my face. I dabbed on some fresh lip gloss, trying to erase the look of defeat away. I held out my hands and the shaking wouldn't stop. "I give up. Fuck it."

I was surprised to see Supreme standing in the middle of the hallway when I came out the bathroom. "Where have you been? They called in the studio a half hour ago saying you were here."

"Baby, the guy gave me the wrong studio. I sat in the lounge for over fifteen minutes before someone told me the correct one. By that time, I had to use the bathroom. I'm sorry I had you waiting."

"That's cool. I just worry about you. All these vultures around here, I would hate for one of them to take you away," Supreme said, kissing me on the forehead. "What the fuck is that nigga doing here?" I looked up and saw Mike.

"Precious, I see that you found Supreme."

Supreme eyed me suspiciously.

"Baby, studio A, the session that Mike is in, was the wrong room I accidentally went into. Mike was nice enough to point me in the right direction. Thanks again."

"I was happy to help. Supreme, I hope there's no hard feelings about what went down the other night; I heard your bodyguards were in pretty bad shape."

"Nah, they recovering nicely, but I got two more here with me, until they back a hundred percent. Would you like to meet them?"

"No, I'll take your word. But with a girl as gorgeous as Precious on your arm, you might need a few more. It would be ashamed for someone to come take her away."

"Nigga, stay away from her." Supreme and Mike were now standing toe to toe.

"Supreme, stop. Let's just go. He didn't mean nothing by it." I was holding onto Supreme's arm, praying he would back down. He had no idea he was butting heads with a stone-cold killer.

"I think you should take your woman's advice."

I finally got Supreme to walk away, but not before

Mike said, "Precious, I'll make sure to tell Nico you said hello."

"Who is Nico?" Supreme stopped me and asked.

"Nobody important. Just some dude that we both know from Brooklyn."

"Precious, I don't ever want you talking to Mike again. If you see him go in the opposite direction, 'cause that nigga rubs me the wrong way." Supreme didn't have to say anymore, I had already come to that very same conclusion.

Imperfect For You

For the third night in a row, I woke up in a pool of sweat, suffering from the same nightmare. I'm at a funeral and my mother, Bree, Nico, Ritchie, Butch, Azar, Tommy, Porsha and Inga are all there dressed in black. I'm the only one in white.

I walk over to my mother, but it's like she can't see me. No one can see me. I'm invisible. Then they all gather around the casket that is about to be lowered into the ground. I slowly move forward to get a glimpse of the person we gathered here to mourn and to my horror it's me. I blamed Mike for my delusions, and it made me angry. In a twenty-minute conversation, he managed to turn my whole world upside down.

A loud knock at my bedroom door, helped shake my terror by bringing me back to reality. "Come in, Rhonda."

"You left your phone on the couch last night.

Supreme's calling you," Rhonda said handing me my phone. "I'm sure this is one call you don't want to miss," she smiled, closing my door.

"Hi baby."

"You still in the bed, sleepyhead?"

"I'm getting up now."

"What you doing later on?"

"Hopefully I'ma see you."

"Cool 'cause I wanted to take you out to dinner tonight."

"Really, where?"

"You'll see. All you need to do is show up looking your beautiful and sexy self."

I was thrilled Supreme planned a romantic outing for us. I could now focus on something other than death.

After speaking to him, I had the energy to get out of bed and eat some breakfast. "Good morning, Rhonda."

"Good morning. Supreme called pretty early today."

"He wanted to tell me that he planned a romantic dinner for us tonight."

"Nice, things have gotten really serious between you all."

"I know, so serious that I think it's time for me to sit down and let him into my life."

"What do you mean?" Rhonda raised an eyebrow seeming confused by my statement.

"I'm somewhat guarded about my life. I don't trust people, and because of that, I keep most things to myself. That way no one can hurt me. But since I've fallen in love with Supreme, I want to share my world with him."

"That's sweet you're willing to be vulnerable. It sound like you're in love. I hope you and Supreme have a wonderful life together."

"Me too. There are a lot of things about me that you don't know and neither does Supreme. After I give him a glimpse into my world, I'll know if we have a future together. I can only pray Supreme loves me enough to forget about my past and focus on our future."

"You sound so passionate. I would feel compelled to forgive whatever you've done in the past, and I don't even know what it is."

"Rhonda, this isn't funny."

"I wasn't joking, I'm serious. I'm impressed you're putting it all on the line and opening up to Supreme. Most people would be afraid. I could always tell that you were different, but I didn't want to intrude in your life. You appear to be perfect on the outside, but you've made it clear that the inside is a lot more complex. But I'm glad we met. You've had such a positive influence in my life."

"Thanks, Rhonda. You pretty cool yourself. You did take me in as a roommate without even knowing me."

"That's called desperation, and the fifteen thousand dollars upfront didn't hurt."

We fell out laughing because it was the truth.

"I'm glad I was desperate though, because you turned out to be the best roommate ever. You're unlike any friend I've ever had. You're just a genuine person. Your feelings, thoughts, are all so real. In my world those qualities are an endangered species. I'm keeping my fingers crossed because I truly hope that everything works out for you and Supreme. I want the two of you to live happily ever after."

"Me too."

I spent the rest of the day preparing for my evening with Supreme. I went and got my nails and hair done. My silk press was laid. Even with the humidity, no revert in sight. I took Rhonda with me so we could both get pampered with a deluxe spa treatment. Then I got waxed up, so my skin was smooth like a newborn baby. By the time we got home, I had a little under an hour to get dressed. I put on a silk, deep V-neck plunged white dress, that had rhinestone detailing, which added a little sparkle. It was backless with three delicate butterflies on the lower back cinching the waist. The length fell right above my knees and accentuated every curve. It was giving high class rich bitch vibes.

"Damn. When Supreme sees you in that dress he might ask you to be his wife tonight," Rhonda said when I pranced in the living room.

"Girl, you so crazy."

"Call me crazy if you like, but you look like a goddess. No one would ever guess you can handle a gun better than a dude."

"Let that be our little secret," I winked.

"Do you know where Supreme is taking you?"

"Not yet." I was giving myself the once over in the hallway mirror when the downstairs concierge called up.

"Your Prince has arrived," Rhonda announced. I grabbed my purse anxious to see Supreme. "Have fun tonight," she said blowing me a good vibe kiss.

"I will." I couldn't get downstairs fast enough. Once outside, my chariot awaited me in the form of a Rolls-Royce Phantom Scintilla, in ceramic two-tone finish with white on the top and an exotic blue color at the bottom. The driver was holding the backseat passenger door open for me and Supreme stepped out with the most beautiful bouquet of flowers. He had on a linen white suit, which matched perfectly with my white dress. A tear rolled down my cheek, but this time it wasn't out of pain. It was pure love.

Between making out with Supreme in the backseat like we were in high school and being in awe of the tiny hand placed optic stars arranged in a wavy pattern on the leather roof lining, I didn't pay attention to where we were going. So, when we arrived at what looked to be an airport, I was confused. "Baby where are we?"

"Teterboro Airport."

"What are we doing here?"

"They're fueling up the private jet. We're having dinner on the beach in Barbados."

"Are you serious? I've never been on a private jet before or dinner in Barbados. I can't believe you're doing this for me."

"I wanted this night to be special."

During the flight I kept pinching myself because this couldn't be real. My life seemed to be going too perfectly: no drama with bitches, no drama with my man and nobody getting killed. It didn't seem like my life; it was like I stepped into someone else's, which was fine with me. I welcomed the change.

When the jet landed, a car was waiting to take us to a yacht. Then the yacht took us to a private beach. A path of rose petals led to our table in the center of a glass gazebo where we would have a romantic dinner. The gazebo was surrounded by vandella roses and pink peony flowers. Flat dishes filled with sand displayed vanilla candles. A mini orchestra dressed in tuxedos was playing the most soothing music. We slow danced and Supreme held me closely in his arms. It felt dreamier than a Hollywood fairytale movie.

Once it was time for dinner, there was a full wait staff to serve us our meal and keep the champagne flowing. Coming from the bottom I never imagined what heaven was like, but this had to be it. "Supreme, I never imagined this could be my life."

"It is and it can always be this way. I'm in love with you, Precious. I want us to spend the rest of our lives together."

"Wait," I put my hand up stopping Supreme from continuing. "Before you say anything else, there's something I need to tell you."

"This sounds serious."

"It is. And if I don't tell you now, I don't think I'll ever have enough nerves to do it." I stepped back and took a deep breath. "I'm not sure where to start."

"The beginning would be fine."

"It's a little more complicated than that. Let's go out by the beach. We need some privacy."

I was fighting within myself the entire time we were walking towards the beach. It was this persistent loud voice in my head begging me not to reveal my secrets to Supreme. It wasn't until the very last second did I make my decision.

"What do you need to tell me, Precious?" staring in Supreme's eyes almost made me change my mind. I didn't want to lose him, but I knew it needed to be done.

"It's only fitting that I purge my soul in the middle of paradise. I'm not making excuses for my choices, but I shared with you what my childhood was like. Because of that, I got caught up in a lot of bullshit, and I became cold. When you in the streets, nobody gives a fuck about you. I was just trying to survive and maintain. During that time, I eventually met a man by the

name of Nico Carter."

"Nico, is that the guy Mike mentioned when we were in the studio that night?"

"Yes. I lied when I told you he was nobody. Nico Carter is actually my ex-boyfriend who is currently locked up doing life in prison for a murder I set up."

"What!"

"He cheated on me, humiliated me and made me look like a fool, and I wanted to teach him a lesson. Some might say I took it too far, but I was a different person then."

"Wait a minute...Nico Carter. I remember that case. That happened not too long ago. His trial was in the paper almost every day. He was some major drug dealer from Brooklyn. He was convicted of double homicide. They said it was over some drug deal gone bad, but you're saying it wasn't that at all."

"No, it wasn't. It was all my doing. I started having sex with his best friend Ritchie and made sure he found out, so that he would kill him."

"He killed his best friend for fucking around with you, but why the other guy?"

"He didn't kill Butch, I did. Ritchie partnered with Butch to take Nico down. Butch murdered my previous boyfriend Azar. So, when the opportunity presented itself, not only did I get revenge against Nico, but I also got revenge against Butch for killing Azar. Nobody knows that but you, Supreme. Nico probably has his suspicions, but he has no way of knowing for sure. He also believes I took a million dollars from him, which I did. I wanted the money to leave Brooklyn and start a new life."

"How does Mike fit into this?"

"I guess when Nico and Mike were both in the drug game, they were business associates. That night I ran into him at the studio, he was supposedly delivering a message on Nico's behalf."

"And the message was what?"

"When Nico gets out of prison, he's going to kill me."

"Didn't he get two consecutive life sentences?"

"Yeah, but Mike sounded so sure that death was knocking at my front door."

Like it did the first time Mike delivered Nico's threat, my heart began racing as I replayed the warning he gave me. His words left me terrified. I did not want to die. Supreme came towards me and wiped away the tears streaming down my face. He held me in his arms.

"Precious, don't worry. Mike was just trying to rattle you."

"It worked. I never thought another world existed outside of Brooklyn that I wanted to be a part of, but I was wrong. I know I've lied to you, and you have every reason to turn your back on me, but just know that you're the first man I've ever loved, and I want you to be the last."

Supreme released me from his embrace and went and sat down on a large rock near the water, putting

distance between us. I knew there were so many other secrets I was leaving out, but I didn't want to overload him. I just wanted to paint a clear picture of who I used to be. Plus, no matter what, some secrets have to die with you. I mean I had changed, but the streets of Brooklyn would always be in my blood.

The longer Supreme sat in silence deep in his thoughts, had me thinking the worse. I walked over to where he was sitting. I had to know if we had a future together.

"Can you please say something...anything."

There was a heavy sigh and then a moment of stillness before Supreme spoke. "I'm glad you were honest with me, Precious. It explains why it's difficult for you to let your guard down. Now that I know what you've been through, all I want to do is protect you and take care of you. I could never turn my back on you. What you just shared with me, only makes me love you more because it shows courage."

Supreme stood up and faced me. I was about to embrace him for understanding and not judging me, but he put his hand in his pocket and pulled out a tiny black box. Before what I thought he was about to do sunk in, he got on bended knee. My whole body started shaking, overwhelmed by what I believed was about to happen next.

"Precious, you're the only woman for me. I want to spend eternity with you. Would you do me the honor of becoming my wife?"

Remember when I said I came from nothing but was determined to have it all? That meant designer clothes, foreign cars, some diamonds and furs. You know the material things that all project chicks want. See, that was my hood dream.

When I rep'd for Brooklyn I had all that. Niggas couldn't tell me it could get no better. Every bitch in the streets wanted to be me. I was Nico Carter's girl. We were the King and Queen of the hood. All mother-fuckers had to bow down. I had my kingpin, so having it all had been accomplished in my book.

But now, here I was relaxing on a beach that I arrived at on a yacht and before that a private jet, and Supreme, one of the biggest Rappers in the world, who I was madly in love with asked me to be his wife. So, I'll admit it. I was wrong. There is more to life than being 'Hood Rich'.

"Of course I'll marry you, Supreme. I love you more than anything in this world."

Supreme slid the massive diamond engagement ring on my finger. We held each other and then our passionate kiss turned to us making love on the beach underneath the moonlight. My life was finally at peace.

Kiss Of Death

When Supreme and I got back from Barbados, I started planning our wedding immediately. The manner in
which he proposed to me was so romantic that I wanted our wedding to be on the beach, too. I preferred
a small ceremony, but Supreme wanted something
extravagant. We compromised and decided to meet
someplace in the middle. I didn't have anyone to invite
but Rhonda so the guest list would be comprised of all
of his family and friends.

A week after we got back from our trip, Supreme
took me to meet his mother and father, who also lived
in Jersey. Supreme was originally from Queens, but
once he started getting to the bag and closing major
deals, he bought his parents some big boy regal type
estate in the suburbs. Spending time with them made
me optimistic that me and Supreme could grow old
together.

Their only reservation about our upcoming nuptials was that we were both so young, but they said as long as their son is happy then that's all that mattered. And it was obvious how happy Supreme, and I were together. Having their blessings meant so much to me. They truly were the sweetest couple and embraced me as if I was their own daughter.

At the same time, being around Supreme's parents revived the painful memory of losing my mother. While I was packing up the last of my belongings, I picked up the only picture I had of my mother. In the photo she was holding me when I was a baby. I pressed the picture frame against my chest and closed my eyes. In that moment I felt she was right here with me.

In the photograph her face glowed and she appeared to be full of happiness. I can never remember a time growing up when my mother was healthy and drug-free, so I always held on to this picture because it was my proof that my mother loved me. Her life was stolen from her when she was still so young. It didn't seem fair.

I often found myself staring at her picture for hours, looking for clues as to what went wrong. How did a woman that had the capabilities of having it all, live her life as though she was nothing? I wondered if she was looking down on me and knew how happy I was. How I wished she could be here to enjoy this with me. Planning my wedding, meeting my future husband and being a grandmother to the child I hoped to have

in the future.

"My beautiful mother. I pray you have forgiven me. Right when you turned your life around, it was taken away because of the decisions I made. Hopefully turning my life around will be payment in full and give you the peace you deserve."

Speaking those words out loud made me believe they would reach my mother. I kissed her beautiful face in the picture and glanced around my bedroom one last time feeling nostalgic before walking out to the living room. Rhonda was standing by the window gazing out at the New York skyline view. As if feeling my presence, she turned around.

"I can't believe you're moving out. I miss you already, Precious. I know you can't be married and living here with me, but can't you wait until after the wedding to move out."

"I'ma miss you too, but my fiancée wants me to be with him. I love saying that by the way," I smiled.

"I bet you do. You're marrying Supreme. And the wedding is in a few weeks. Talk about moving fast. I feel sad, but you're one lucky bitch," we both laughed.

"I am a lucky bitch. And yes, I'm super excited about this new chapter in my life with Supreme, but I'm still gonna miss you. I really do have a lot of love for you, Rhonda."

"And me for you."

We stood in the living room hugging it out. I was going to miss this apartment and living with Rhonda.

We really did become friends, and I had a soft spot for her. But it was time to close this chapter of my life. I was about to move on to my happily ever after with Supreme.

It seemed like overnight it was the day of our wedding. With all the planning I did to have the event take place on a beach, we ended up having an elaborate ceremony right in our own backyard. With the growing guest list and celebratory parties people threw for us, it didn't make sense to try and fly everyone out to a beach. Plus, the mansion we lived on had more than enough space to accommodate the lavish affair.

After we exchanged vows, took pictures and had our first dance to *Halo* as husband and wife, I came upstairs to change out of my wedding dress. Although it was beautiful I couldn't wait to step into the custom designed dress Supreme had made for me. I was admiring how exquisite I looked in my wedding gown one last time in the three-sided floor-length mirror when I caught a glimpse of someone I never wanted to see again.

"You really are the most beautiful bride I've ever seen." Mike stood there completely fixated on me.

"How dare you show up here!" I could not contain my disbelief and fury. "You weren't invited to this wedding. How did you even get past security?"

"That was an oversight. I'm invited to everything."
I wanted to smack the smug expression off his face.

"That was no oversight. What do you want...to
deliver another message?" I was doing my best to contain my rage while trying to get Mike the fuck out.

"As a matter of fact, yes. Nico said congratulations
on the nuptials."

"Oh really. So, you ran and told him I was getting
married?"

"Actually, he read about it online and when I
spoke to him, he asked me was it true. You know he
still loves you."

"GET OUT!"

"Calm down. You shouldn't get upset on your
wedding day."

"Then leave!"

"I will, but only if you allow me to kiss you goodbye, on the cheek of course."

I remained motionless as Mike came closer to me.
I figured if I could tolerate playing along with his psy-
chological game for a brief moment, he would leave
and perhaps stay out my life permanently now that I
was Supreme's wife. He kissed me on the side of my
cheek, making my skin crawl. But what he said next
had me ready to crash out.

"Till death do you part," Pretty Boy Mike whispered in my ear, then vanished out the door as quickly
as he appeared. I fell to the floor in my wedding dress
fighting back tears.

Take It In Blood

You know they say every time a child is born someone has to die. I pondered what man or woman would sacrifice their existence in order to breathe life into my child. A month after Supreme and I got back from our honeymoon, I discovered we were pregnant. That's how he liked to think of it. I would remind him, though, that while *we* were pregnant, I was the one waking up every day with morning sickness.

I'd never seen Supreme happier than on the day I told him I was carrying his child. Sometimes life can be too perfect. I woke up to Supreme rubbing and kissing my stomach. That was his daily routine ever since he found out I was pregnant.

"Good morning, my little man."

"Little man? How you know it's not my little princess?" I countered.

"My gut is telling me them back shots I gave you

produced my little man, that's all."

"Them back shots? You're a mess!" I grabbed a pillow from the bed and kept playfully clobbering Supreme over the head.

"Yo, yo, yo, enough," he laughed, grabbing the pillow out my hand. "It don't matter though, whether my little man or your little princess, it's nothing but love. I just feel blessed my beautiful wife is giving me my first child."

"I'ma do my best to be a good mother. I want our child to have the life I never did."

"Baby, you're going to be a wonderful mother. This child's life is already starting off different than ours."

"But you have great parents."

"I do. I was blessed to grow up with both my parents, but they had to break their backs to provide for us. I could've easily turned my soul over to the streets, but this music game was my savior. That's why when you made your confession to me, I didn't judge you or think any less of you. I know what desperation can make you do."

"You're right. I've seen firsthand what desperation does to people," I said thinking of my mother.

"Desperation is real. Most people fold and either get strung out on drugs, commit suicide, end up in jail for doing foul shit or even lose they mind. Then they might as well be dead because they just floating through life anyway with no purpose. But your desperation gave you determination, and I admire you for that."

"With all I've seen in my life, I've never been one to have a lot of faith in God. But now I know that prayers can be answered because only God could've brought a man as amazing as you to me."

"I feel the same way about you. I'm blessed that I can take care of you the way you deserve, and our child will never struggle the way we did." Supreme put his arms around me as we laid in the bed close to one another.

"The only thing I wish, was that my mother was here to see how my life turned out. She would know that dreams do come true."

"She knows," Supreme said kissing me on my forehead. "I'm sure your mother is smiling down watching over you and our baby."

"Today is actually her birthday. I think I'll go visit her final resting place."

"Do you want me to come with you?"

"That's sweet of you to offer but I need to do this on my own. I haven't been there since she was first buried. But the next time I visit, I would love for you to come with me. Having your support means everything to me, Supreme."

"You're my wife and I will support and love you unconditionally."

That morning Supreme and I began making love with a newfound intensity. With every thrust our bodies engulfed one another as if holding on for dear life.

It was as if we were making love for the first and very last time.

When I arrived at the burial site, I took a moment to appreciate the beautiful tombstone Bree picked to honor my mother. She had it engraved with exactly what I asked: *A Fallen Angel Who Is Now Forever At Peace.* I laid the flower arrangement down and while praying, I felt somebody walking up behind me. I dreaded coming to Brooklyn. When I first pulled up to the cemetery, I even sat in my car for a few minutes seeing if I observed anyone or anything suspicious. I hesitated to turn around and see who was walking up behind me.

"Precious, is that you?"

I tilted my head to get a glimpse at who was calling my name. To my relief and surprise, it was Bree.

"Bree, how are you?" I stood up and gave her a hug, genuinely happy to see the woman I considered a mentor in many ways.

"I thought that was you. I've been trying to get in touch with you, but the number I have was disconnected. I was hoping you would be here today since it's your mother's birthday."

"I changed my number and lost all my contacts. Are you good, is everything straight with the detail shop?"

"Yes, I'm good, this is about you."

"About me, what is it?"

I could see the grave concern on Bree's face "I wanted to warn you."

"Warn me about what?"

"A week ago, while at the shop I heard some guys running their mouths. They mentioned your name. They said Nico Carter was getting out of prison soon and the first person he was coming to see was you."

"You must've misunderstood. Nico is doing life in prison. That's a mistake."

"No, it's not a mistake. They said he retained some new heavy-hitter appeals attorney that got his conviction overturned on a technicality. He should be released any day now."

"You must've misunderstood them. Maybe they were talking about another Nico," I stuttered, trying to catch my breath.

"I see you're upset. Please come sit down, Precious."

"I can't. I have to go, Bree," I said mumbling over my words. My whole body went weak. I leaned on my mother's tombstone to maintain my balance. I was in denial, refusing to believe anything Bree was saying.

"Precious, are you gonna be alright? Please sit down on the bench so we can talk."

"I need to find out how much time I have before Nico is released. I have to go!"

"Precious wait!" Bree yelled out to me, but it was

too late. I got in my car and sped off trying my best to run away from the truth. I took off my baseball cap and freed my hair, hoping it would eliminate the migraine headache I was now suffering.

My mind was spinning. Bree said Nico would be getting out soon, that meant he was still locked up and I had time to get to the bottom of everything. I thought about trying to get in touch with pretty boy Mike, but I had sworn to Supreme that I would never speak to him again. *Maybe Rhonda could speak to Mike for me and see if he had any information about Nico's release,* I thought.

I needed to talk to someone who could calm my nerves and come up with a solution. The only person I thought of was my husband. I immediately called Supreme.

"Fuck!" he didn't answer so I left a voicemail. "Baby, I'm on my way home. Please meet me there as soon as possible. I need to talk to you about something really important. I love you."

Being out of Brooklyn and back in New Jersey put me somewhat at ease. As I drove up to the gate, I turned around in every direction feeling someone was following me. I knew my nerves were raw and my paranoia was on overdrive. Once the gates closed behind me and I was home, a sense of relief that I was now safe came over me. I looked down and placed my hand on my stomach. I began talking to our baby who was growing inside of me, knowing it would bring me a sense of serenity.

"Everything will be alright, my angel. Your daddy will make sure of that. He'll come up with the perfect solution," I said pulling up to the circular driveway and parking in front of the estate. Maybe he could pay Nico off, or if necessary, have him killed. However it went, I knew Supreme would work it out. Or so I thought. My whole life seemed to move in slow motion after stepping out my car. There stood the ghost from my past. Only it wasn't a ghost. I blinked my eyes, praying my mind was playing a sick trick on me.

"You've done very well for yourself. I'm proud of you, Precious."

I closed my eyes tightly. I continued to try and convince myself when I opened them the nightmare will end because Nico would not be standing there.

"Baby girl, open your eyes, I'm not going any-where. I'm the real deal."

"Nico, you can't really be here."

"You're just as beautiful, if not more, than the first time I saw you walking the streets of Harlem. I knew you didn't belong there. Now look at you, married to a superstar, living in a mansion. You made Brooklyn proud. The problem is, you sacrificed my freedom so you could gain all this. Now it's time for you to pay the price for what you've done."

"Nico, please! I was immature back then and I

made a huge mistake. But I'm a different person now. I've put the streets behind me and turned my life around."

Nico began clapping and mocking what I said with his applauds. "You turned your life around, but you sold me to the devil in order to get it. Not once did you think about the life you took away from me, and the money you stole. You destroyed everything we had over a bitch I didn't even give a fuck about. But that didn't matter to you, because you're like me. Your pride and your ego dictate your moves."

"I'm so sorry. What can I do to make this right? I can give you back the million dollars and even more money than that."

"The only way you're going to make this right, is by me taking your life."

"Hasn't there been enough death in our lives? I have a husband, Nico and I'm pregnant with his child. I'm living a life I never dreamed was possible. Don't take that away from me. I don't want to die."

I couldn't have stopped the tears from flowing even if I wanted to. I had convinced the world that I was strong for so long that I almost fooled myself into believing I was invincible. But here I stood the most vulnerable I've ever been, pregnant and alone. "Please don't kill me Nico," I begged one last time for my life and the life of my unborn child.

"You're already dead. I just came to take it in blood."

Nico reached in the back of his pants and retrieved his gun. He raised his weapon. We both turned our heads when we heard Supreme pulling up.

Supreme's eyes zoomed in on the gun Nico was pointing at me. He jumped out the moving SUV and ran towards me. His bodyguards jumped out too, close behind him with their own guns raised. But it was too late. The loud explosion ripped through my chest. The pressure jolted me back, and I hit my car before falling down to the ground. Then I heard Nico shooting in the direction of Supreme and his bodyguards as he vanished into the darkness. Supreme ran to me cradling my limp bloody body.

"Precious, baby, it's me Supreme. Please stay with me. The ambulance will be here any minute. Baby, please hold on."

I struggled to keep her eyes open. "Supreme, I'm so happy I was able to see your face one last time. Baby, I love you. I never knew what love was until I found you. Please forgive me for leaving you and taking our baby too."

"Pease don't leave me," he cried out in unbearable pain, stroking my hair. Supreme kissed me on my forehead. I could feel the warmth of his arms holding me tightly. But as my blood continued to flow, my strength deteriorated, and my body wanted to be at peace. The last words I heard before my eyelids shut was Supreme begging God not to let me die.

Read The Entire Bitch Series in This Order

ORDER FORM

Name:

Address:

City/State:

Zip:

QUANTITY	TITLES	PRICE	TOTAL
	Bitch	$17.99	
	Bitch Reloaded	$17.99	
	The Bitch Is Back	$17.99	
	Queen Bitch	$17.99	
	Last Bitch Standing	$17.99	
	Superstar	$17.99	
	Ride Wit' Me	$17.99	
	Ride Wit' Me Part 2	$17.99	
	Stackin' Paper	$17.99	
	Trife Life To Lavish	$17.99	
	Trife Life To Lavish II	$17.99	
	Stackin' Paper II	$17.99	
	Rich or Famous	$17.99	
	Rich or Famous Part 2	$17.99	
	Rich or Famous Part 3	$17.99	
	Bitch A New Beginning	$17.99	
	Mafia Princess Part 1	$17.99	
	Mafia Princess Part 2	$17.99	
	Mafia Princess Part 3	$17.99	
	Mafia Princess Part 4	$17.99	
	Mafia Princess Part 5	$17.99	
	Boss Bitch	$17.99	
	Baller Bitches Vol. 1	$17.99	
	Baller Bitches Vol. 2	$17.99	
	Baller Bitches Vol. 3	$17.99	
	Bad Bitch	$17.99	
	Still The Baddest Bitch	$17.99	
	Power	$17.99	
	Power Part 2	$17.99	
	Drake	$17.99	
	Drake Part 2	$17.99	
	Female Hustler	$17.99	
	Female Hustler Part 2	$17.99	

QUANTITY	TITLES	PRICE	TOTAL
	Female Hustler Part 3	$17.99	
	Female Hustler Part 4	$17.99	
	Female Hustler Part 5	$17.99	
	Female Hustler Part 6	$17.99	
	Princess Fever "Birthday Bash"	$6.00	
	Nico Carter The Men Of The Bitch Series	$17.99	
	Bitch The Beginning Of The End	$17.99	
	Supreme...Men Of The Bitch Series	$17.99	
	Bitch The Final Chapter	$17.99	
	Stackin' Paper III	$17.99	
	Men Of The Bitch Series And The Women Who Love Them	$17.99	
	Coke Like The 80s	$17.99	
	Baller Bitches The Reunion Vol. 4	$17.99	
	Stackin' Paper IV	$17.99	
	The Legacy	$17.99	
	Lovin' Thy Enemy	$17.99	
	Stackin' Paper V	$17.99	
	The Legacy Part 2	$17.99	
	Assassins - Episode 1	$12.99	
	Assassins - Episode 2	$12.99	
	Assassins - Episode 3	$12.99	
	Bitch Chronicles	$40.00	
	So Hood So Rich	$17.99	
	Stackin' Paper VI	$17.99	
	Female Hustler Part 7	$17.99	
	Toxic...	$12.99	
	Stackin' Paper VII	$17.99	
	Sugar Babies...	$12.99	
	Deadly Divorce...	$12.99	
	The Legacy Part 3	$17.99	
	BITCH The Story of Precious Cummings	$17.99	
	Mastermind	$12.99	

Shipping/Handling (Via Priority Mail) $9.85 1-3 Books, $18.40 4-10 Books. For 11 or more $24.75.
Total: $_____FORMS OF ACCEPTED PAYMENTS: Certified or government issued checks and money Orders, all mail in orders take 5-7 Business days to be delivered